THE LAST WHITE MAN

Books by Fadhil Qaradaghi

Novels in Kurdish:

The Holy Boar (2006)
The Warlock of the Village (2007)
The Bigs and the Littles (2008, 2018)
(Under the title: *Come Back Home Our Beloved Stork*-2008)
A Murder in the Cretaceous Period (2018)

Nonfiction in Kurdish:

Ancient History of Kurdistan (5 Books)
Other Nonfiction in History, Religion, and Thought

Novels in English:
The Bigs and the Littles (2016)
A Murder in the Cretaceous Period (2017)
The Warlock of the Village (2018)
The Last Day of Sodom (2019)
The War of the Witches (2022)

Fadhil Qaradaghi

THE
LAST
WHITE MAN

A Novella

ZAGROS BOOKS

2023

To Charleston
Despite everything that is happening here

Whites, Reds & Blacks

For the Lord, your God is God of gods and Lord of lords, the great, the mighty, and the awesome God, who is not partial and takes no bribe.

Deuteronomy 10:17

But the Lord said to Samuel, "Do not look on his appearance or the height of his stature, because I have rejected him. For the Lord sees not as man sees: man looks on the outward appearance, but the Lord looks on the heart."

1 Samuel 16:7

"God does not show favoritism."

Romans 2:11

And one of His signs is the creation of
the heavens and the earth and the variation
in your languages and colors. Verily in that
are signs for people of knowledge.

The Quran 30:22

God created Adam from a handful He
took from throughout the Earth. Hence
the children of Adam came in accordance
with the Earth: the White, the Red, the
Black and the others in-between; the easy
and the rough, the evil and the good, and
the others in-between.

A speech attributed to
Prophet Muhammad.

Stop it, Mother. The Blacks, too, are your sons. Did you forget that Jesus was a man of color?

Reverend James Waring
Charleston, 2048

Great and first in many things, Charleston. And so, I'll give you the honor to conquer before all.

Leo Quinn, the last White man in the New
Confederacy
Charleston, 2049

CHAPTER I

Leo Quinn pulled the jacket hood over his eyebrows and held it tight with two fingers. A gust of April's wind could push it away and expose his head to the sky and ruin everything. Although unsure, Mercy Ray could reverse its effect and change him back to his Black self. That was the last thing he wanted; at least for now.

He loved to look up at the unseen spot in the space in which the satellite swam. But there was no need to do. The little baby was doing its job, calmly reflecting its ray over this large part of the country.

A genius invention to force the exchange of skin colors, he thought.

As Joseph Wragg's horn blew a long blast, announcing the ship's voyage across the Atlantic, the audience responded with yells of joy.

A few months ago, the owner of the little ship had renamed it after the eighteenth-century Charlestonian leading slave trader.

Now, Wragg was doing the reverse operation: sending the Blacks back to Africa.

The cries of the Black women and children aboard the ship followed the sound of the horn and grew louder with the second long blast. The Black men hurled insults at the White crowd who responded with whistles.

The crowd of Whites was made up of ordinary people, police officers, reporters, and punks. But because of their flags covering the scene, the White supremacist groups appeared more, and also dominant. They shouted repeatedly, drowning out the cries of the Black people on the ship.

South Carolinians were the majority while the rest were Southerners and others from outside the Confederation. And many foreigners, as Charleston was the tourists' favorite.

All groups were committed White supremacists. Despite differences in organization and details of thoughts, they overlapped in ideologies and strategies:

Neo-Confederates, who formed the majority of the organized groups and clung to Christian culture were more than the others. National Socialists, and more broadly; Neo-Nazis. Fascists. Identitarians. Satanists. Other Far-Right groups; not affiliated with any of the previous ones. Skinheads of many groups. Even a few tiny groups like The Kshatriyas, who revived the ancient "Aryan" history, were present.

There were also "moderate" racists with the ideology of racial separation —instead of racial superiority— as a better choice for every race.

Most of those were unorganized and independent pro-Confederation people forming the majority among the racist population. Moderates —good or evil— always formed the majority in every society.

Many of those moderate racists described themselves as proud Christians.

Europeans; namely members of chapters of this or that American organization, were also among the attendees celebrating what all agreed to call Liberty Day.

In addition to flags representing White supremacist groups, flags of a dozen different categories fluttered: The Confederacy. South Carolina's the Palmetto and the Crescent. Charleston. This or that county. And human symbols as well: posters of the Confederacy's heroes, White combatants from the past decades and, expectedly, The Führer. Banners with slogans like "Liberate the Aryan Race." YWNRU, and its longer form: "You Will Not Replace Us." This was also a song a cluster of people was chanting.

"Lots of extremist and armed groups," Quinn said to himself. "One of the socio-political laws says that you guys will soon fight each other. But I'm going to save you from that fate."

Some of the Black women aboard lifted their White babies. The Whites on the shore responded to their appeal with laughter. Then they shouted the German, old anti-Jewish cry of the eighteenth century, now for the Blacks, with a dull, quick rhythm: "Hep hep Niggers! Hep hep Niggers!"

The babies weren't White. They were hybrids resulting from the rape of Black women by some brave White men. Those infants bore much more Black blood than the one-drop rule would accept one to be White.

Quinn spotted who appeared to be Native Americans; at least two of them. A White group must have caught them hiding since they had deported all the Indians to the cities outside the Confederacy. South Carolina did the same to the enslaved Indians more than three centuries ago.

Without waiting for the green light from the authorities, White supremacists embarked on a project that both, they and the authorities, had planned.

They launched widespread raids to terrorize "the enemy" who was a broad range of targets including migrants, Blacks, Jews, anti-racism activists and occasionally, Catholics.

The authorities allowed only some ethnic and religious groups, which the White supremacists referred to as "Replacers," to relocate to the states outside the Confederacy. Other groups were sent back to their countries of origin. Black Americans were denied the opportunity to replicate the Great Migration of the twentieth century and had no choice but to relocate to a country in Africa that was promised as a "Black Heaven."

Southern White supremacists were not the only groups seeking to rid the country of Black Americans. Other states also frowned upon the possibility of a new Great Migration. Many Blacks themselves refused to relocate and follow in the footsteps of their twentieth-century peers.

Meanwhile, Jewish Americans recognized that they had no future in the United States. Their leaders pleaded for deportation when Neo-Nazis began targeting them.

The Jews left America, but not for Israel which was destroyed during a war with Muslims after an influential branch of the Evangelical church, Israel's former ally, withdrew its support.

Those Evangelicals, who supported the American White supremacist president, sought to bring about Armageddon and the Second Coming. They allied themselves with White Nationalists to force American Jews to gather in Israel which then would be the fulfillment of the prophecy.

For their part, the Nationalists had a long time ago described Israel as an occupation and spoke out against the "Jew-controlled governments in the world" and called for "kicking the Kikes out of the world." They first worked to kick them out of the country.

After getting rid of those they deemed inferior races, this place on Earth felt it deserved a celebration of a victory she hadn't seen since two centuries ago as South Carolina, and especially her first capital; Charleston proved to be the place of grand actions in the remote past. Quinn could recall many of them:

First, it was the struggle of the State's old colony to survive attacks from Indians, Spaniards, and French. Her successful engaging in a massive slave trade. Then fighting stubbornly in the Revolutionary War against the British. Her generosity when relinquished her right to be the capital of the Confederacy to Richmond, Virginia. And the first shots in the Civil War were fired in Charleston when the Confederates bombed Fort Sumter, the Union fortress, across the town's harbor.

And when the war ended, South Carolina suffered the greatest percentage of losses in men and wealth in the entire country, all in support of the Confederacy's cause. The state lost six to seven percent of her White population and more than eighty percent of her wealth. She was the most despised state by federal soldiers for being the starting point of the secession plot.

Charleston was the Grand Dame; not only in war, revolution and rebellion; but also in wealth and prosperity. And in the modern age, she so attracted tourists she ranked as the number-one city to visit for many years. Her famous delicious food. Her slow rhyme of life Quinn loved. And rich with preserved historical sites and buildings. And with a sky free from skyscrapers hiding or even dwarfing those ancient buildings. Churches and steeples everywhere. And the first building in America to serve solely as a theatre; the Dock Street Theatre. And other number-ones.

And now, South Carolina and Charleston were at the center of Quinn's grand project that would impact the New Confederacy. Despite the impending disaster that he was about to inflict on the city and the State, he believed he was honoring them with this great change.

In Quinn's opinion, Chucktown deserved more honor than he was giving her. Every Charlestonian held her in high esteem, but Quinn's eyes saw her as even greater.

Like the old pirates arriving from the sea, Quinn landed in Charleston from the heaven of fate, fully aware that history would change from here.

Charleston always amazed him, while the other parts of the Confederacy were to him only orbits around her. She was his first option when he sought a strong rival. Then he briefly abandoned her for Richmond, the former capital of the Confederacy, before returning to her once again. And he canceled her again and then back to her. Eventually, he settled on his Charleston. He looked like a gladiator roving about the world on a hunt for a competent rival to conquer. And he found that in Chucktown.

Quinn feared one thing: firstly, he hated her, but with the progress of his project he feared he would love her before he could accomplish the project. If it weren't for her growing racism, he might have fallen in love with her. But no! She was now his peer in a coming great battle.

The last cargo of deported Black people was leaving. And ironically, most of them were descendants of native Black Charlestonians, while only a portion of those who celebrated their departure were native Charlestonians. A long time ago, transplants had become more numerous than Charleston natives.

Initially, Quinn attempted to blend his transplant accent with southern words and dialect. But this made no difference as it wouldn't harm his project. As a transplant, he was welcomed in Charleston unless trying to change things. This was Charleston's rule for transplants. Quinn's goal was to bring about a single change that would trigger a sequence of changes, all while remaining anonymous as the planner, whether a native or a transplant.

Despite his extraordinary project, Quinn's personal history was modest:

Leo Quinn: Born in 2015 in Charleston to parents also born in the city. His father's grandparents had moved to Charleston as early as 1983. Spent most of his time in New England.

Another horn blast jolted him back to his current time and place. Wragg's cargo was small compared to the ones that preceded it. It was small but symbolic: a cargo departing from onetime Gadsden's Wharf.

And another symbolic structure was here: the International African American Museum once occupied space on the wharf. The building stood there, but now as Hampton Confederate Museum; a new museum that the City Council added to the other Confederate museums.

Two and a half centuries ago, here in this place, the most horrific phase of the slave trade was going on for two years. From 17 February 1806 until late December 1807, Charleston benefited from an ordinance the city's council passed that granted Gadsden's Wharf exclusive rights to receive ships importing African slaves. This made it the last and the most important place for disembarking African slaves in North America.

Today's celebration of the Whites was to end the paradox of the past. On one hand, slave labor made the country prosper. On the other, it made Black people the majority in the state during the eighteenth century and until 1930. It was the glorious history of the White Man, but also its aftermath. And now, it was Charleston taking the lead in rectifying the latter.

"Zero Niggers" was the slogan of the new White supremacist movement in what were known as the Slave States and now the New Confederacy. The Zero Goal had been achieved; zero Negroes in the states except for those lynched in some public squares. Their hanging bodies served as a warning to any rebels who dared to refuse exile. The ideology of White supremacy stated that the good Black was the deported Black or the dead.

The Whites didn't call it an exile. Following the example of Liberia, the new country for Black Americans was a land in Africa called Gabon. Perhaps it was the original home of their far ancestors; at least for some. But for the White people, it didn't matter if it was Gabon or Niggerland. To them, all were Niggers came from Africa. They called that country that almost all of them never heard of "The Black Haven." But the Gabonese, for their part, never heard of such a Heaven, and when the deported Blacks arrived, they heard the natives simply referring to the country as Gabon. The Black Haven, the idea and the name, was a lie that many of the Whites didn't feel it was necessary to mention. Just deport them; it was that simple.

But why Gabon? Why not any other African country?

Quinn was so preoccupied with his invention at the time that he didn't pay much attention to geography or politics. Later, when he learned the reasons behind the choice, he realized that it had no bearing on his plans. France, the old exploiter of Africa, backed a government it installed through a coup. America backed the opponents. With White supremacy growing stronger in America and French secularism becoming more aggressive toward cultural diversity, Gabon was chosen as the exile for Blacks by the former and for Blacks and Muslims by the latter.

When the exiled Blacks and Muslims arrived from France, a new coup led by pro-Americans overthrew the Gabonese government.

Confederacy supporters in the federal government and legislature pushed for the coup. When it lost its territory, France suddenly remembered that deporting Black people by its rival was inhumane. But the plan kept moving forward, and fully loaded ships crowded the Atlantic heading for the compulsory paradise.

To ensure a smooth procedure, White supremacists leveraged the resources of the Union and pressured the federal government into signing a contract —a word of mouth, in fact— with the new Gabonese dictator to accept Black Americans in exchange for economic support for the country and political one for the dictator.

The country received only a fraction of the former, and even that went to the dictator, along with full political backing.

Quinn knew the rest of the story since it was his project:

The Whites re-established old groups like The Redshirts, The White League and others. Some emerged to the surface without passing through the underground phase. The Ku Klux Klan was still active but was old-fashioned compared to the new groups with charismatic leaders.

The groups became increasingly angry at what they thought to be discrimination against the Whites. They mixed hate speech with bitterness toward the media and government, both focusing only on the crimes of Whites. The groups portrayed the country as one having an oppressed majority of Whites and a minority of superior people of color. They marked 2050 as the year when they would become the minority, and America would become Black.

And to fuel the fear of a coming Black rule, the groups revived the memory of "the misery of the White Man" during the Reconstruction era when Blacks gained control in the South after the Civil War with the backing of the federal government and army.

Then the White groups went a step further and pushed the Republican Party to adopt an extreme-right ideology.

They lobbied the GOP to nominate a populist businessman to run for the presidency. In return and when the President; he used his two terms to fuel hatred against immigrants at first and then against people of color. The new president rewarded the White groups by condoning their expansion, especially in the Upper and Deep South, then allowing them to infiltrate the government departments. They had infiltrated the police a long time ago before that.

On the other hand, the increasing alignment of the Democratic Party with homosexuals and transgender people pushed the moderate conservatives to the Republican Party and the right-winged movement that defended family values. Some adopted the right-wing ideology, while the majority became more indifferent to racism. Both parts reached the point at which they said: if the price of keeping the family and its values was driving out the Blacks from the country, then let them do it.

The White groups soon evolved from elite-centered to popular forces all over the country until they gained control in the Southern states. One of the old slogans of days of bitterness: "Separate Country for Whites," was quickly forgotten and replaced with "America for Whites only." Then as everybody expected it, they formed —or revived, that was how they loved to describe it— the Confederate States. The New Confederacy was born, but without seceding from the Union, though.

Continuing to call back history, the White supremacists lashed out at Whites outside the Confederacy who defended the Blacks and called those Whites "Neo-carpetbaggers." And they intimidated and silenced similar southern Whites, calling them "Neo-scalawags." This was reusing the derisive term the old White Democrats —when Democrats were southerners and racist— used for White southerners who stood with the Blacks and supported the Republicans. The White supremacists even assassinated a few southerner White activists.

Remembering those victims, Quinn knew they would consider him worse than a scalawag if they knew about his project.

The widespread movement to revive Black culture and learn the Gullah-Geechee language was an opportunity for White supremacists to spread a conspiracy theory about a coming revolt like the alleged one of Denmark Vesey in the early nineteenth century.

All that was the last phase of preparing for the genocide which was conducting massacres until they could force the Blacks out of the country. A wave of attacks began against Blacks living in mixed neighborhoods, along with lynching

Black men here and there and molesting Black women. Black mobs responded with riots, causing further damage. This gave proof to the conspiracy theory and led the White militias to change their strategy. They attacked the Black quarters and burned their houses, making this a daily routine. The police, now almost entirely infiltrated, stood by, and sometimes joined the militias.

This was the outline of the story, necessary for Quinn to justify his project. Additional details only added bad to worse. One detail was the date of the last cargo of Blacks that would appoint the day to celebrate the victory.

In early December of the year before last, eight of the twelve members of Charleston's City council proposed December 20th of that year; 2047. On that day in 1860, the South Carolina General Assembly voted to secede from the Union due to slavery matters and became the leader of the rest of the southern states and the spearhead for the coming Confederation. That would have made the date of the last cargo of deported Blacks coincide with the 187th anniversary of the State's secession.

It was The Palmetto Regiment Group, the most prominent White group in South Carolina, who suggested this date to also meet almost exactly the 195th anniversary of forming the historic Palmetto Regiment that fought bravely in the Mexican war.

The other members and some of the legislators —who thought of themselves wiser than their peers— considered the date too close, and so; a too impetuous —and also provocative— step.

They also rejected two other dates that offered a longer span of time: February 8th of the next year, 2048, which was the anniversary of forming the old Confederacy in 1861 by the first seven slave states. April 12th was the second suggestion that commemorated the attack on the Union force in Fort Sumter that started the Civil War. They found the former even more provocative and the latter extremely aggressive.

A serious problem with all three dates lay in them being unrealistic and impractical. There was still work to do to deport all the Blacks since some continued to resist. This was right. The situation on the ground in 2047 needed more violent operations and more time and could have continued throughout 2048.

Having soldiers and officers from the army among them —and fewer numbers from the National Guard— the Black men had organized themselves into armed squads and companies. They patrolled their areas day and night and this changed White groups' raids on civilians into clashes between armed forces.

In most areas, the Blacks lost their jobs and suffered from poverty and even starvation. This pushed them to change their strategy from self-defense to conducting counter-raids to provide their families with food and other necessities of life. And when a Black attack was the case, the police pushed more units to the White militants' side.

White lone wolves and organized Accelerators shot White rallies with sniper rifles or handmade bombs to frame the Blacks and spark the impending civil war.

Here and in every Southern state, the governors waited for the situation to worsen to justify sending in the National Guard. And when they finally did, one could distinguish between the White militias and the National Guard only by the nuances of their uniforms.

Eventually, April of the next year, 2049, won the contest. It wasn't Fort Sumter's April 12th, 1861, but a memory more related to the recent deportation of the Blacks:

On April 10th, 1877, after months of a dual government and legislature —Republican and Democratic— the federal army company occupying South Carolina's State House in Columbia was ordered to withdraw. The Democratic members of the General Assembly, known as the Wallace House, took their seats as the legal house. The following day, Wade Hampton III, a prominent politician and a significant slaveholder who led the White supremacist redeemers, was inaugurated as the lawful governor, replacing the Republican governor Chamberlain. This marked the end of eight years of Black and radical White Republican dominance, backed by the federal army, in the State.

It wasn't a forgotten day in the New Confederacy because high schools taught it. Hence, it came as no surprise when a teenager in a high school proposed it as the day for celebration.

The New Confederacy waited for this last cargo to hold celebrations. It named the day beforehand: The Day of Liberty. The liberty from the Black race. But To justify it morally, at least on Sundays when they went to church, they also described this liberty as a gift to the Blacks.

"A mutual benefit" was the expression Dorian Loyd, the leader of The Palmetto Regiment used in a public speech. Many accepted it, but only to forget it later and stick to the original meaning. Loyd was the first to forget it and simply denied ever saying such nonsense when reminded of it.

CHAPTER 2

The ship still showed in the sea, but Quinn no longer wished to watch it. Although the protective substance of the thin, soft helmet had passed the test he had made on a sample —on himself, in fact— he thought it was safer not to stay under the bare sky for too long. It could be risky even indoors. He still wasn't sure.

The substance needed more tests on many people. But this wasn't part of his plan. Everyone should have been exposed to the ray and nobody would have worn the substance. No one to be spared, except for him. It was Mercy Ray. Thus he called it.

As to Charleston, maybe ninety-nine percent of her people would take their share of Mercy Ray outdoors since the city had events and festivals all year round. Charleston's March that Quinn chose to expose the South to Mercy Ray had a rich calendar of events. Then April would bring further festivals. The people enjoyed about a dozen events in those two months:

The Wine and Food Festival. Front Beach Fest Isle of Palms. The Festival of Houses and Gardens which would extend for three weeks. Catholics —now mostly became White supremacists— held the St. Patrick's Day Parade; a single-day event but with a more than one-mile path under the sun in which every foot would take its share of Mercy Ray. And other events. Most interesting was the Cooper River Bridge Run, about good six miles of a running event with walkers in the back half.

Every festival continued in Charleston and its county during the past years except those of the Blacks and Caribbeans: Charleston Carifest, Charleston Caribbean Jerk Festival, Sweetgrass Cultural Arts Festival, and especially the Moja Arts Festival. All had gone forever with the Blacks.

Quinn needed at most a couple of months to protect himself. He could manage to spend the longest part of that period wearing the hood at home. Two months indoors were a small price for the drastic change he hoped. But it would be more endurable if he wore a lighter object.

One mile separated him from the house he rented in Radcliffeborough; a neighborhood named after a small-scale slave trader. His way passed through Wraggborough neighborhood that was named after Joseph Wragg.

A parade of The Redshirts marched ahead of him. Passing by what once was Emanuel African Methodist Episcopal Church, or shortly Mother Emanuel Church, to go to Radcliffeborough wasn't inevitable. He could leave Calhoun Street at its intersection with Elizabeth Street on the right. Then he would walk along the latter and make another turn, now to the left, into Henrietta Street. Then the third turn to Meeting Street, down along Marion Square, to get back to Calhoun Street and reach Radcliffeborough.

Names of slave owners and slave traders and their children, he thought to himself. *But there are more streets and squares and they'll think of naming the rest after the slaveholders' dogs.*

Quinn knew it was an exaggeration, but why not?

He could take that path, but he kept his way on Calhoun Street and followed the parade. They had returned from the port and were raising flags of the group and the Confederacy and South Carolina. Armed men with red shirts. Women and little girls with red ribbons in their hairs, red wristbands, or a red tie under the collar. Boys held toy guns.

Mother Emanuel Church of the past decades lay on his right. Next to it, but some hundred feet closer to him was a little park in which Black men were hanged in a row from the trees. As the bodies outnumbered the trees along the street, the Whites hanged the men in twos and threes from one tree.

All were young men except for one old man with a white mustache and a white, thin circle beard on his square chin. The silence of the corpses stood at odds with the din of the parade. The Whites whistled and booed, then said insulting words, and always raised their flags and waved them. Quinn thought they meant the dead men. Then he noticed they were looking at the right side of the street.

The church he used to attend was the oldest Black Methodist Episcopal church in the South. It suffered from the White groups burning it more than once; each time a group of them. The Blacks abandoned it, partially destroyed and burned, a few months before the city deported them. And to prove their religious tolerance, the City Council, submitted it to a church that the more committed Christians called a heretic church; namely a Unitarian.

James Waring, the new pastor; a White in his mid-forties, asked the Black people, now fewer than ever, to attend his church. He gave sermons about love and equality in the eyes of God.

Curious Whites also now and then came to take a look at the building and to hear what the priest would say and then ended up protesting his sermons. They sat separately inside, and later bullied the Blacks outside, and then never came back. They never believed that God meant them to be equal to Blacks. Every race was equal to itself. Even the less interested in churches and religion didn't see that Blacks had the right to attend churches with Whites.

Other Whites agreed with the words of Reverend Waring, but they feared angry Whites, so they chose silence.

It's a matter of time, Quinn thought, watching the Redshirts parade. *Threats today. Acts tomorrow.*

He felt sorry for the pastor for the harm he would cause him.

Forgive me, Father Waring. You don't deserve it. You always stood with the Blacks against inhuman and non-Christian injustice.

Waring wasn't alone. Quinn knew that. Many people refused racism, but the White supremacists silenced them like the good attendants of this church. To Quinn's bad luck, his invention would transform the good and the bad equally. Mercy Ray was man-made had no means to separate one from the other. There was only one thing to do which was to give the secret of the protective shield he wore. But this meant a quick failure of his project.

Or suppose I tell them about it, he thought for the hundredth time, *will they believe me?*

Pushing his hands into the pockets of his rain jacket, Quinn walked faster past the parade. And again, staying under the sky was unnecessary. It sent a light shower that would end soon as usual. But this made no difference. Mercy Ray would penetrate the clouds and drop with the rain.

Marion Square lay to his right, bustling with activity. Farmers used to bring their goods every Saturday from April to November each year in what was a long time ago the Charleston Farmers Market and also on Saturdays and then additional Saturdays and Sundays in December before Christmas.

It was Saturday and the farmers were there with their tents, selling a variety of fruits and vegetables and artisan goods. The latter, surprisingly, were Gullah handicrafts they had bought, or even robbed, from Blacks. Jolly music expressed the new Feast of Liberty. Maybe there were also the usual performers somewhere in the park. Today was a double event. All seemed happier than the last year and the year before last and the one before it, and many other years before.

But he felt happier than them. It was his day, not theirs. And here he was in the square to eat something. No. Lots of things. Not fruits or vegetables, but dishes; preferably traditional.

There was a table selling the famous traditional shrimp and grits, which the label read that it was of African origin. They didn't feel embarrassed to mention it. When it came too food, races were tolerated. Another African: "crab rice" of Gullah-Geechee origin. And a third African. Then Quinn read Frogmore Stew, a dish named after a place, and without frogs; the label said. And many others without labels. One 'without' was a barbeque, but he wanted it without the usual mustard sauce.

He wished he could eat everything put on every table. Charleston was renowned for her traditional foods. And today was her day of celebration.

He felt full as a tick before he left Marion Square to his temporary home; a small house he rented in Radcliffeborough. Quinn had shifted there as it was safe and affordable and with small shops. And bars and restaurants. Longtime Charlestonians dwelt there. And many college students and professors from the Medical University and other students from College of Charleston. And also artists. And fun, although he stayed away. It was a vibrant area, especially at night.

Quinn opened the door and stepped inside. The doorway split his body into two parts: inside and outside. This reminded him of the basis of his invention: every human being held the genes of every race and color; the dominant genes and other weak genes. The White Man was White because his white gene was dominant, but he had all the other color genes, all hiding until something could make them prevail.

A kind of ray he discovered could do that. One day, this idea sprang into his head and he formed its logical equation in a few minutes, but finding a way to embody the idea took him two years.

His first test was the last year; on the eve of 2048. He used a device he installed in a workplace occupied by four men. It consisted of directly exposing a White to the ray from the device. The ray transformed the man into Black, but it also affected his office mates and turned two of them to dark brown and one Black man into White: Quinn himself.

Quinn then could have installed the device on his car to test it on other people. More tests were necessary, but more results also meant turning the transformation into a public case that the health department should have studied. Each of the two tests worked in one month and the isolated transformation cases passed publicly unnoticed.

The next necessary step was broadcasting the ray from a satellite to cause a mass effect. Would this have worked? "No" needed more work in unfavorable circumstances, while "Yes" meant changing history.

He waited one year to expose Charleston to the ray. Until this time, he invented the protective substance and when it was time for Charleston and the South; that was on March 10th, 2049, a few Blacks were waiting to be deported. Starting before that date meant transforming the Blacks when still in the city. It would have caused a great shock for the Whites. He would have enjoyed the shock, but stirring up the Whites for an unnecessary change was also unnecessary. And maybe risky.

Although there were still a few days left to complete the one-month transformation period, Mercy Ray transformed Black infants before time.

Quinn smiled when he heard the Whites mocking the Black mothers, not knowing what surprise fate held for them. Those Black children would grow up and see their White peers turned Black. The event of people exchanging their colors was great fun and a breakdown of the Whites' arrogance at the same time. The Black-to-White change was coming.

Mercy Ray began to reap the white gene. But Quinn had a question he asked himself whenever he ended his day. He repeated it now while still in the doorway:

"When all turn to Black and I become the last White man," he said, "will the ray reverse its effect?"

"It'll be funnier," he went on. "Two successive repeated seasons for the people here: let's say, six months of black skin and six months of white skin."

He smiled again.

"Lamenting for the six black months and joy during the six white months. And after a few years, when they get used to this round and what'll be up next, they'll lament up front in the first month of the white period."

The doorway was still splitting him into two. He ended his thoughts and went in, walked toward to the mirror and stood before it, unzipped the jacket and pulled back its hood. It bothered him to remember he had to wear it. Delaying the project to summer with the hood on his head would have meant enduring heat and humidity and endless questions and suspicions.

"This hood would've been at odds with Charleston's summer except for its frequent rain," he mused. "It'd be like wearing a cassock and worshipping both God and a superior race at the same time."

Putting on a rain jacket to hide the protective material was the main reason to begin his project in spring. Although rain fell in every season including spring, the season's mild weather wouldn't raise many doubts about covering his head. On the other hand, it might stir up a question for the White people —after becoming Black— about the hood's possible connection with him staying White. Most bothersome was wearing the jacket indoors, at least as a precaution since he still wasn't sure of the extent of the ray. A broad hat could fit, but only for half of the head back.

He reached inside the hood and touched the layer covering it.

"Even though wigs are thin, they may do the job," he said. "The film is so thin and transparent it can stick to the wig easily. And a wig cheats the curious people of all seasons."

Quinn decided to finish this little, but important detail before he could enjoy the effect of his invention. The satellite was now relaying the ray that Quinn broadcasted from an earth apparatus to a large circle of lands in the Confederate States. And for good measure, Quinn had exposed the houses of White supremacist leaders to extra bands of the wave from his car.

Now, throughout the whole month that had passed, the South was in the grip of a satellite broadcasting a merciless ray that had the power to turn upside down the life in the Confederacy and the entire country, and maybe the entire world.

CHAPTER 3

Dorian Loyd's phone rang amidst the hurrahs of the crowd who were waving the flags of the Confederacy and South Carolina and The Palmetto Regiment. The latter considered itself the heir of the South Carolinian unit of volunteers in the American-Mexican war.

At first, Loyd didn't hear it because of the clamor. Carl Dylann, the leader of the armed brigades of the group —a huge man with a black beard and black eyeglasses and always holding a rifle— leaned in his ear.

"Your phone, sir," the man said.

"Sorry," the White leader said. He smiled at the audience who gathered to hear from him the news they knew beforehand.

They took the opportunity of his short silence to chant a version of Dixie's song:

Southrons, hear your country call you!

Up, lest worse than death befall you!

They continued the song while Loyd was taking the phone from his pocket to see who it was.

Hear the Northern thunders mutter!

Northern flags in South wind flutter!

Unknown caller.

To arms! To arms! To arms, in Dixie!
Send them back your fierce defiance!
Stamp upon the cursed alliance!

So, it wasn't worth answering, especially on such a glorious occasion. He canceled the call, smiled again and put the phone back into his pocket.

Shoulder pressing close to shoulder!
Let the odds make each heart bolder!

Loyd lifted a hand to them to listen. They stopped singing. Others in the back continued the song in a low, thunderous voice.

"Our New Confederacy became the example for what the other parts of the United States should be," Loyd resumed his fervent speech. "We worked for a nation with one race, one blood, one color. We saved our Whiteness. We thought we'd be lucky if we could deport the Replacers without having to end their lives except for only a few of them. And we—"

The phone rang again before he could say that they did it. He pressed his lips together with frustration. His phone insisted. Waving their flags in great arcs outward, the crowd shifted to the common Dixie song:

I wish I was in Dixie!
Hooray! Hooray!
In Dixie's Land, I'll take my stand!
To live and die in Dixie!

Couples began to dance Carolina shag.

Loyd took the phone again from his pocket. The same phone number. Now he noticed it: the code of work phones, not personal. This would make some difference.

The throats still chanted the anthem:

Away, away, away down South in Dixie!

Away, away, away down South in Dixie!

Yet, he hesitated to answer. Tom Schultz, his deputy, got closer.

"You better shut off the phone," he whispered.

"One moment, Tom," Loyd said, tapping then the device to accept the call.

"Dorian!" the voice of a man said. "I'm callin' you from the hospital."

Loyd recognized the voice. He was Doctor Stanley Barns, his friend and the science theorist of the group.

"Hey, Stan!" Loyd said. "Don't tell me Ashley died while giving birth to the baby."

"She's fine," the doctor said. "Or, maybe not. But the baby—,"

Loyd cut him off.

"Died? Doesn't matter," he said and ended the call and shut off the phone.

"One baby died, a nation was born," he said as if talking to the doctor.

Loyd spoke to his audience for a few minutes before his deputy's phone rang. The sound bothered him.

"Tom!" Loyd said to his deputy without turning to him.

With the phone raised to his ear, the man understood and moved away from his boss. He stood behind the white banner that mildly fluttered in the breeze and bore the famous fourteen-word-slogan that many groups used:

"We Must Secure The Existence Of Our People And A Future For White Children."

"Yes," Schultz whispered into the phone.

"I'm Doctor Stanley Barns from the hospital, Mr. Schultz. I know you're there," the voice on the other end said. "Dorian's wife made a baby."

"Good news," Schultz said in a low voice. "He thought it died. I'll tell him later."

"No. Tell him now," the doctor said, firmly.

Schultz wondered why it was a doctor calling him not a nurse. And he was a close friend of his boss.

"No way, Doctor," he said. "It's the most important speech in decades. He's recording a new history. Would you please understand me?"

"The news I brought him is more important than any speech he'd ever give," the doctor said. "Dorian is recording history there, but it's the history reversed here in this hospital. It may undo his entire project. I'm sure he'd hope his wife had died."

Schultz paused for a few moments.

Doctor Barns exhaled. "I tell you, and you tell Dorian and I bet he won't dare to tell anybody," he said.

"Then say it quickly," Schultz said.

The doctor said only one sentence. Schultz's face turned pale and he ended the call without saying goodbye. He squeezed the phone until he thought he had crushed it. With a stiff gait, he moved toward his boss, pushed aside Carl Dylann who stood right behind him and leaned forward.

"It was the hospital," Schultz said with a throaty voice. "You got a baby."

"So, it didn't die," Loyd said, smiling at his audience. "Okay, Tom."

The crowd slowly swayed and rocked on the sides and chanted South Carolina's old song:

Call on thy children of the hill.

Wake swamp and river, coast and rill.

Rouse all thy strength and all thy skill.

Carolina! Carolina!

"Look at me, Dorian," Schultz said, dryly. "It isn't okay. Ashley gave birth to a Nigger baby."

The crowd's voice echoed, louder and quicker with their new slogan:

White Carolina! White Carolina!

* * * * *

Loyd walked with wide, angry steps toward the recovery room. Dylann followed with his rifle. Both arrived, Loyd entered and Dylann stood outside the room.

Loyd's wife lay on her back, looked at the ceiling and cried. A Black baby, wrapped with a white cloth, lay on a little bed beside her, sleeping deeply. Loyd turned to face the female doctor. He read the name badge on the doctor's white coat.

"So, Doctor Jameson, you were so kind-hearted you fed an animal," he said.

The doctor said nothing. Loyd crossed his arms on his chest.

"Whom should I ask for an explanation?" he asked. "You or her?"

"The three of us must explain it," the doctor answered.

"You mean it could be my fault?"

"One possibility among others."

"And so, the possibility relating to me is that I may have at least one-eighth Negro blood that came to me from some Negro ancestor."

"Everything's possible, even if she admits it was her fault," the doctor said.

"Or you maybe changed the baby," Loyd said. "What do you mean by 'even if she admits it was her fault'?"

"You know there are no Negro people here," the doctor said, holding up the DNA test chart. "It's your baby, Mr. Loyd. We did the DNA test."

Loyd gaped at the chart.

"I don't know what those things on the paper are," he said. "So, it's a lie. Or maybe a joke. Somebody wanted to spoil my great day."

"You can do the test at any hospital you choose," the doctor replied.

Loyd looked down and squeezed his forehead.

"The baby's yours, Dorian," another voice said.

Loyd looked up. Doctor Stanley Barns stood behind Doctor Jameson.

"And what was it, Stan?" Loyd asked. "A mutilation of the baby's DNA?"

Barns shook his head helplessly.

"Then a drop of Black blood in Ashley's ancestors," Loyd suggested.

"I hope you can convince the people of it," Barns said.

"This or that," Loyd said, crossing his fingers. "There's a lie that we should bury. Come in Carl and take this creature."

"This's what you should do," Barns said, leaning down to hold the baby.

All three moved to the door. Ashley, so far lying down and listening, looked at the sleeping baby in the arms of the doctor and sighed with grief. Her husband turned to her.

"Don't tell me it's the heart of a mother?" he asked.

She turned the other way and said nothing in reply.

When in the garden, Loyd held out his arm to Barns. The doctor tightened his arms around the baby.

"Not here, Dorian," he said.

"It should be here, Stan," Loyd said. "The lie should be buried where it was born."

Barns gave him the baby. Loyd rolled his arm around it and stretched the other hand to Dylann to hand him the rifle.

Barns wagged his finger. "Again, not here, Dorian," he said.

"Again, it should be here. I'll take responsibility. If there'll be any."

"There'll be none," Barns said. "I just don't like to see blood in this garden."

"Black blood is dripping in every garden and square in the country, Stan."

Loyd looked at the baby with questioning eyes. He thought of waking it up and then hanging it on the tree with its swaddle blanket. His friend would not agree. Taking the baby to a public garden or a square wasn't an option either. That meant enduring a time with the Black creature in his car, which was more than he could stand.

Dylann stretched his hand with the rifle. "I can do it," he said. "One bullet in the head is more than enough."

"Not a bullet, Carl," his boss said. "Doctor Barns doesn't want to see blood in the hospital."

Dylann nodded. He hung the rifle on his shoulder, and with a firm smile on his face, he grabbed the baby by the legs and swung it for a while.

The yell of a man on a loudspeaker from outside came loud and savage, "Hospitals won't see again Black animals born."

"No, they won't," Loyd said in a low voice. "This was the last one."

The leader of his armed brigades swung the baby faster, moved his arms with it stronger the last time and beat the tree trunk with it. The baby cried once and for the last time.

Dylann let the dead infant fall on the ground. Loyd looked at Barns with a smile of contentment on his face.

"You see, it ended without a drop of blood," he told his friend, dusting off his hands.

"It did, Dorian," Barns said, gesturing his head to the tree.

Loyd turned to it. A red thread ran down the trunk.

Barns beckoned to two nurses on the other side of the yard. Seeing everything from their place, they hurried to the spot. They kneeled and wrapped the baby's body with its white cloth. One poured water on the tree trunk while her friend went to bring a bin, and then came back running and pushing a wheelie bin. The first dropped the body into the bin and the other continued her way, hurrying.

"Take him to Hell," Loyd told her.

"She was a girl," the young woman said, turning over her shoulder.

Suddenly, Loyd felt a sharp pang in his brain. It took him a moment to recall the face of a little girl —his first child— who had died when she was only one month old.

"Makes no difference," he said at last, then in a low voice as if talking to himself, "The death of an infant of a superior race is an important event. The deaths of other infants are equal to the death of an insect."

He smirked at the doctor. "We'll see what will become of Ashley," he said before walking away.

He savored the fading sounds of the parade, repeating the men's slogans with a martial rhythm. Then he cursed the Black girl who had ruined that part of his day.

Loyd got into the back seat of his car, still cursing under his breath. Dylann ordered the driver to move. They passed by a parking car beside the hospital fence. Loyd saw the driver with a hood on his head. He vaguely remembered the driver being there when he had arrived at the hospital. The eyes met, but Loyd was so preoccupied he forgot the matter when his car moved a few yards away.

Quinn didn't. He had an inkling that something was off about this sudden unexpected visit but decided it was too early to celebrate just yet.

CHAPTER 4

News spread about the wife of the strongest White supremacist leader giving birth to a Black baby. Footage taken from a hospital surveillance camera showed Dylann smashing the newborn's head against a tree while Loyd and hospital staff looked on.

The newborn surprised even Quinn although he had given a double dose of Mercy Ray to some of the White leaders. He had stayed near the hospital to ensure that Loyd's wife did not miss any more Mercy Ray sessions. But it happened quickly, confirming his assumption that the ray affected not only existing human beings but also embryos, sperm, and ova.

Loyd was less concerned about the crime exposed to the public than he was about his future as a pure-blooded white leader with black genes in his family tree. He contacted Dr. Barns before discussing his wife's case with his colleagues.

"I want you to change the DNA tests," Loyd told him. "Later, I'll kick Ashley out of my life. I'll pay for a private flight for her to join her tribe in Gabon."

"It ain't that simple, Dorian," Barns replied. "Someone could expose the test results. Don't forget that someone leaked the hospital footage."

"So, you still have hybrids in your hospital. Right?"

"No, not necessarily. It might could be a White with what they call 'real Christian creed' or 'humanitarian philosophy' or any other nonsense."

"So we need inquisition trials. This's a promise I'll make to my followers. Of course, after I get rid of my problem."

"Give me the rest of the day to see if I can fix it," Barns told Loyd.

For the next three hours, Loyd waited anxiously for his friend's call, refusing to watch the news or answer the flood of calls from friends and followers. Breaking every contact with the outside world was his choice for the moment. He sat in his chair, tapping his thigh with his right hand.

Finally, Barns called him back. Loyd jumped to his feet.

"Are you still alive, Dorian?" Barns asked.

"Go ahead and give me the good news."

"Hmm. Did you watch the TV channels? Any one of them?"

"No."

"There is news. Good or bad? Only the devil knows. Maybe both good and bad. And in every case, you may need to put both the DNA and Ashley on the shelf for now."

"Say it, man. Say it quickly."

"Similar cases have appeared around the country. White mothers made Negro babies. At least I'm sure of a dozen cases; one in Athens—"

"Athens?" Loyd interrupted.

"Athens in Georgia, Dorian," Barns explained.

"Oh, I see. Then?"

"Then many others. To tell you the names of the cities won't do anything for you. You just need to know that your case wasn't unique. Some happened before. They hid it while yours was published. Bad luck struck you before everyone, my friend."

Barns waited for Loyd to comment. A heavy minute of silence pressed on his nerves.

"Dorian! Are you gaping?" he asked.

"I am," Loyd answered while slowly sitting back down.

"You can call it frenzy. You can call it panic. You can imagine the unimaginable. The country's holding its breath."

Loyd remained silent for a moment before finally asking, "So that's why a thousand people contacted me and each made a thousand calls?"

Barns didn't respond. Loyd stood up and turned on the TV, flipping to his channel, The White Revival, which was covering the situation like it was World War Three. He laid his cell phone on the table, not hearing his friend asking if he was still there.

The TV channel showed what the doctor had described: frenzy here and panic there. Reports were overwhelming the channel about new cases. So far, one thousand cases, most of them happened in the past few days when the parents and the hospitals reported them. Loyd's Black baby encouraged others to disclose their cases. It seemed like a plague beating the country. In some cities and towns, White militias attacked the houses of Black newborns, looting and burning them.

Zach Martin, Loyd's favorite correspondent, was covering the attacks. Trying to justify the assaults, he was picking his words. Those attackers, he explained, fought who betrayed the nation for not admitting their Black ancestors.

Loyd muted the TV to take calls, spending two hours repeating the same message to everyone: this was a disease or even a plot, and he would never let it pass.

As Loyd was on the phone with Barns again, Zach appeared on the TV screen, glaring. Loyd lowered his phone.

"The Health Department's press conference was canceled," Zach said, nervously and moving his free hand. "Instead, a statement was released. The epidemic, or the plague, or the curse, or whatever you call it, is widely present only in states of the Confederacy.

Adjacent states have recorded some cases. And many other cases have appeared among people in other parts of the US and the world, all of which were visitors, tourists, or businessmen who stayed for some time in this or that place of the Confederacy."

Barns had already told Loyd about these details. The newest was that the Confederacy, the full-blooded White states with zero Blacks, was at the heart of the disaster.

Turning pale, the newscaster could barely muster his words. "It may be a virus that Black people spread before leaving, Zach. Did the Health Department mention such a possibility?"

"Nobody here has any explanation, Joe. All they can do for now is to follow up."

With a shaky hand, Loyd turned off the TV. The remote control slipped from his grasp and his phone fell from his other hand to the ground. He sank down into the chair, crossed both hands on his knees, bowed his head and grabbed his forehead with his right hand.

Barns was still shouting on the phone

*   *   *   *   *

Quinn lounged on the sofa, stretching his legs out on a small table and watching the news. His eyes wandered up to the hood on his head. "With this thing on my head, I can't enjoy watching the live scenes of the coming storm," he muttered, before standing up and walking over to the sink.

He pushed the hood off his head, leaned over the sink and washed his head quickly. Then, he shaved his head with a razor so swiftly that he nicked himself in a few places. When he was finished, he pulled the hood back on his wet head, ready for another outing.

As usual, he walked between the church and the small park, which was now devoid of the hanged bodies. The priest stood in the doorway of the church, crossing his fingers on his chest and looking up. He seemed oblivious to the nervous pedestrians who walked by, shaking their fists and arguing with each other, or speaking on their phones.

The priest recognized Quinn from his pale jacket hood and smiled at him. Quinn didn't miss the bitterness in the smile.

"Good afternoon, Father Waring," Quinn greeted him.

"Good afternoon, Leo," the priest replied.

"No more blood," Quinn said. "Thank God."

"Thank God," the priest echoed.

So, the priest hadn't been watching the news that was setting the country on fire, Quinn concluded. Even the agitated pedestrians didn't seem to pique his curiosity. No wonder. He had stopped his sermons and had withdrawn to a room in his church, disconnecting from the outside world. He had assumed that the people were excited about deporting the Blacks, even though none of them had shown any joy.

The church stood in stark contrast to the world around it. It was a monotheistic, ardent anti-racist church. While many Catholic priests and some Protestants shared Waring's beliefs about racism, they were all silenced. They were even persecuted, much like the Black community.

The short conversation was more than enough for Quinn. His need for a wig was urgent. Finding a suitable one that matched his old hair color and cut wasn't easy. Without this, he needed to dye it and change its shape.

At the big market, Quinn surprised the salesman when he wanted to try the wigs on in the fitting room, rather than in front of the nearest mirror. The salesman looked up at Quinn's hood suspiciously, as if he expected a head without a skull. Quinn ignored him.

In the fitting room, Quinn tested the wigs quickly. All were an average size and had straps to keep them securely in place. Uncomfortable; yes, but safer. One dark blond fitted both his head and features.

At first, he had managed to attach the protective shield to the bottom of the wig at home, but now he liked the idea of doing it in the fitting room and then walking out with it on.

He had to do it quickly. Now this all-seasons hood was ready to wear.

Quinn returned the other wigs and asked the salesman for a darker wig in the same size and shape as the one he had picked. A spare was necessary.

With her eyes on Quinn's head, the cashier woman smiled as if waiting for him to take the wig off to scan it.

Quinn smiled back from the corner of his mouth and leaned forward, intending to tell her to scan it while on his head. The woman's smile vanished. He straightened and handed her the other wig to scan it and double the price. The cashier smiled again, showing now her annoyance she had to serve such a weird customer.

Take it easy, baby, Quinn thought. Soon you'll see something that makes you forget about this trivial stuff.

Back home, Quinn took a longer path to enjoy the sight of fretted White people.

"Epidemic" was the word he heard most.

At first, White folks accepted the story of mixed blood, but as more Black babies filled the hospitals, they quickly shifted to the theory of an epidemic. And because every supremacist of any kind tended to blame others for every mishap, the conspiracy theory quickly prevailed.

"It happened when the Niggers left," someone told his friend.

Everyone overheard him as he was almost shouting.

Quinn wished to remind the man of the Whites' belief about Black people: they were inferior, underdeveloped and uneducated, and hence unable to create a disease that the developed White community couldn't.

The man's friend replied, "Imagine if we let them stay more than that."

"They would've turned us into apes like them," the other said before both men turned around a corner and disappeared from view.

Quinn wanted to turn around the opposite corner when he heard a woman's scream coming from a nearby building.

The woman dashed into the street as if had seen a ghost. She fell to her knees in the middle of the street and cried.

"No. Not this one, my God," she wailed.

A frightened call from a teenager came from the building, "Mama! What happened to me?"

The cry made Quinn stop in his tracks.

"Oh, no," he hissed. "It has come so quickly."

The teenager ran to his mother and leaned on her, both of them crying.

Passersby stood paralyzed. Some moved backward as if preparing for an escape before the teenager could notice them and then infect them with the disease.

Quinn checked his phone for a news channel. Breaking news stunned him: several cases of teenagers turning black.

"It's working faster than I expected," he said, hurrying then with wide strides toward his area and looking now and then up to the direction of the satellite.

"O, wicked baby!" he said, smiling.

CHAPTER 5

In the days that followed, drug companies, universities, and science centers worked around the clock.

The Medical University, the oldest in the South with a campus in a widespread area in the city, was the first to act. It stopped its classes and dedicated all its resources to what became a census among the experts: a virus had quickly spread and mutated the DNA of the White people resulting in pregnant women giving birth to Black babies.

Quinn smiled contentedly, knowing that the university was only half a mile from him, who was the source of the "virus."

The ordinary man believed more in the leaders of the white supremacist groups than in the scientists. Dorian Loyd declared the situation of his wife, now ex-to-be: she inherited black blood from her African ancestors. And if it was a disease, it did nothing but make that blood surface.

This satisfied the Whites, as they hoped that with pure white blood, their newborns would be rid of the black fate. Loyd and his peers estimated what evil this theory could bring: it would risk crushing the unity of the people of the Confederacy, turning them into two groups: the pure Whites and the Hybrids. However, such a risk seemed more endurable than assuming the disease as a mutilation of every White man's pure DNA.

As expected, the next few weeks brought quarrels in all areas and armed conflicts in some others flared up between the two groups: the intact Whites on one side and the Whites with the Black newborns and transformed teenagers on the other.

Every day of three heavy weeks made new modifications to the map of the two groups. The areas became divided into White and Black zones and were changing their shapes like amoebas. With new Black babies and transformed teens, more families joined the hybrid group and turned them from attackers into defenders.

Throughout those weeks, the scientists reassured the public about the transformation sparing the adults. That was the Confederacy's last hope.

Quinn parked his car next to Loyd's house, operated the device and left the car until the next day. It was the great leader's turn to transform faster by getting the double dose; one from the satellite and another from the device.

But the first black adult came from the other side of the State. Loyd watched his channel that showed Zack speaking to the man whose face was blurred on camera. The man was in tears, lamenting his misfortune, when breaking news flashed across the screen:

A new case: A police officer had transformed into a Black in St. Augustine, Florida.

The third reported case was a seventy-year-old woman. It became clear now that the disease would reveal the hidden black blood in the DNA of people of all ages.

Previous to this, Loyd had lost the wish to speak to his audience. Now, these cases made him afraid to show up to them. During the days that followed, he was looking in the mirror, turning his face right and left to spot any brown little dot on it.

Then he discovered that it was his audience who hadn't the desire to listen. The public's confidence in both the scientists and the leaders was shattered. They lost faith in themselves as bearers of pure White genes.

To the Confederacy's luck, this fear eased the undeclared civil war. The militants withdrew from the streets. All asked themselves: "Who will come next? Will it be me?"

Zach didn't show up for a few days, and Loyd, absorbed in his anxiety and fear, didn't notice his absence. One of Zach's colleagues informed the audience about his mishap .

Stooping over and his face pale, Joe Raymond, the presenter and Zach's closest friend, began the news. He crossed his fingers on the table .

"I'm sorry to tell you that our competent reporter was knocked down by the beast," he said as if declaring an army's surrender.

"It's over," he said, lifting his hand. "We've lost the war before we could even charge our guns. The only thing we should do is sit and wait for our fate. Zach's now waiting to speak to us."

Zach's voice came, slow and stunned while the screen displayed his photo when White with the mike in his hand in front of the Confederacy Presidential office.

Loyd nervously turned around. "Where's the damn changer?" he shouted. He found the remote control, picked it up and turned up the volume.

"It happened, Joe. This's all I can say," Zach said. "But I promise to come back if the channel accepts me."

"What for, Zach?" Raymond asked him .

Loyd's hand was about to smash the remote control. He repeated it, "Yes, Zach. What for?"

"I have now a new message to the nation. We must keep solidarity. We all are Whites. It's a disease and we must stand together to stop it. I'm on my way to the studio."

"Yes, brave man. Yes," Loyd yelled and clouted the air with the remote control in his fist.

* * * * *

Larry John-Ward, the president of the Confederacy, held a meeting with the government and legislative representatives. More than half of the members were now Blacks. The others sat far in the corners with double masks on their faces. John-Ward had turned brown. He wanted to meet them before his complete transform.

"This may be our last face-to-face meeting," he said. "I have no doubt that it's a virus. We must stay at a safe distance. The first thing to do is fund drug companies to find a cure for the affected. Finding a vaccine must begin at the same time."

A White in a corner raised his muffled voice, "First, we need inquisitions. There was hidden black blood in many White people."

"I'd prefer to describe them as blood tests, not inquisitions," the president said. "And they must be compulsory."

"Deport everyone with even one drop of black blood," another White said.

"I'm afraid that it'd be found in most of the attendants here," a dark brown man said.

"Start with me," the president said. "If you find any, I'll pack my bags to Gabon."

"The President knows that we have DNA results of everybody and many of them are subject to the one-drop rule," the man said.

"We still need tests," said a White sitting in the farthest corner.

"He's the representative of a drug company," the president introduced the man.

"As the President mentioned Gabon," the White man said. "We need blood samples from the Blacks we deported to Gabon."

"Didn't I hear someone objecting here and mentioning the DNA bank?" asked the president .

"They showed nothing useful," the representative answered. "We need to search for something new that happened to them. Our scientists reckon that they had spread the virus before leaving for Africa."

"How much funds do you need?" the president asked.

The man scratched his left hand with his right.

"Our proposal is ready, sir," he said.

The president turned to face the attendees as he addressed them.

"Anything that might could help," he said. "If they want the entire budget of the government, we'll give it to them. All public services should stop."

*   *   *   *   *

The news of the meeting leaked, and violence of every kind broke out in the Confederate States. And when unable to find any Black individuals, armed men attacked houses of "scalawags." Robbers looted houses, markets, and public facilities.

Neighborhoods in towns and cities armed their men and women to defend themselves from an enemy that was not clear if was an organized White group or a bunch of robbers. Airports were crowded with visitors trying to leave the area. John-Ward declared a state of emergency all over the Confederacy.

Not waiting for the National Guard or orders from the governor, Charleston's mayor instructed the commander of the Third Coastal Battalion of the State Guard to call upon his unit and inform the Adjutant General only when it would march.

The neighboring states summoned the National Guard that deployed along the borders and blocked them against the now-Black refugees .

*   *   *   *   *

With both elbows on the table and hands around his cheeks, Reverend Waring watched the news.

"No," he said to himself. "It isn't a virus. It's a curse. Even if it is a virus, a curse is behind it. We must undo the wrong we did to the Blacks."

Waring learned about the disaster a few days after he saw Quinn. He now wondered if he was still White and also the same good man.

He walked down Calhoun Street to Quinn's house in the Radcliffeborough neighborhood. Quinn opened the door, and it was a nice surprise. Once in the living room, the priest went straight to the point.

"We were silent about the injustice done to the Blacks," Waring said. "It's time to shout the fact everywhere.

"Maybe I was," Quinn said. "But not you. You always said it to their face."

"It must be more than words said and then forgotten. We must act and form an active resistance. Can you join me? Two scalawags, as they call us, would be the core of the force."

The question distressed Quinn. His project was justice and revenge, and he couldn't withdraw it now. He pushed the thought out of his head. There was nothing wrong with the priest turning black. There was nothing wrong with anyone, especially priests, turning black.

Then he remembered that he hadn't checked Waring's face for brown spots.

Waring noticed his host's eyes.

"Yes?" he asked.

"Sorry," Quinn said. "I was just checking to see if you were turning Black like the others. But I see nothing."

"I haven't thought about it," Waring said .

"Not even looked in the mirror. We can use our whiteness to influence people. They won't listen to a black person, or even a former white."

"I understand," Quinn said. "If we turn black, they'll accuse us of defending the Blacks because we became black ourselves."

Their short conversation made Quinn think about stopping the ray. He became inattentive to the rest of their discussion. He wished Waring hadn't come. And to make matters worse, the priest asked him to return the visit.

"I'd like to have dinner with me in my church," Waring said. "We can continue talking about this."

Quinn wanted to refuse, but it wouldn't be polite.

"Thanks," he said, trying to show a friendly smile. "I'll come over."

Waring smiled in return. "You can even spend the night there," he said. "I promise there won't be a pineapple in your bedroom."

"What pineapple?" Quinn asked.

"Not a fan of traditions?" Waring asked. "Al right. There'll be Country Captain on your honor."

"Who's he?"

"Why! Country Captain, man! Curry chicken. Which do you prefer, onions or garlic or both?"

"Um. Thanks. Neither. Never tried this thing."

"With white rice, whether you like it or not," Waring said, then he nodded and said goodbye.

He walked across the street. Suddenly, he halted and turned around with his entire body. The door was shut tight.

"So strange!" he muttered to himself, "He still hasn't tried the curry chicken. And can't even remember what a pineapple at the foot of the guest's bed means."

He shook his head and continued on his way back home.

*   *   *   *   *

In an effort to forget his discussion with the reverend, Quinn turned on the news after the man left. The first thing he saw was Zach, now with dark brown skin, in the studio.

Only a few sentences from Zach were worth hearing before he shut off the TV.

"There's only one fact," Zach said, beating the table with his fist. "And it's that we're still White. It's a disease the Niggers spread before they left. We'll find the virus and lynch it like we lynched the Niggers in the squares."

As the screen turned black, Quinn lowered the remote control in his hand.

"Sorry, Father Waring," he said. "There's no use. They won't change."

CHAPTER 6

Waring wasted no time. He contacted his churchgoers, urging them to attend the next Sunday sermon where he would present his plan to deal with the crisis.

At the first Sunday sermon, tension was high between the still-Whites and the newly-Blacks.

The aisle separated the two groups. Waring implored them to sit together. The Whites refused and the Blacks insulted them.

Waring began his sermon with its main topic:

"Jesus Christ was supposed to be the savior of the souls," he said, "but the ideology of the devil changed Him to the protector of the color."

The Whites grew increasingly restless as the sermon went on, and half of them declared that it would be their last time attending the church when it ended.

The following Sunday, some of the remaining Whites bullied the Blacks outside the church, attempting to force them to leave. Waring saw the civil war of the country on a smaller scale.

The day's topic was the revenge of God. The few remaining Whites tended to accept the idea but without discussing it with the priest.

Waring stayed alone with Quinn who saw him looking around with eyes full of despair.

"Are you going to quit?" Quinn asked him.

Waring's eyes landed on his friend.

"Never," Waring replied. "I am the servant of God, and I seek His reward even if I fail."

"Then let me give you the good news. Or, it's in fact a conclusion," Quinn said. "A logical ending to what is going on. The Whites who refused your teaching will turn Black and will come to ask forgiveness. Oh, no. Not forgiveness, but prayers. They'll ask you to pray for them to turn back to White. No matter then if God sends them to Hell."

The next day, Waring removed the image of Christ with black hair and light brown skin and replaced it with a Black Christ with curly hair, an image he had been saving for the right moment.

Waring had no clue about the silent protesters now starting to speak out against the injustice the country had inflicted on the Blacks. Their newly declared resistance was met with fierce opposition from those who still believed they were White and would soon turn White again.

On the third Sunday, Quinn's prediction came true. All those who had left the church returned, now Black and bowing their heads to avoid looking at the Black Christ. Only Quinn remained White.

Waring was now light brown. Quinn wished he could spare him, but no one could escape Mercy Ray. Besides, being Black wasn't bad as he always told himself. The Black was equal to the White in the eyes of God.

Among the men and women in the church, only Waring refrained from asking Quinn about his lack of transformation. Quinn repeated one answer: he didn't know, and he wasn't a scientist. But what Quinn truly didn't know was that news of his condition had reached the authorities and the scientific community.

He was worth investigating, but with other Whites in the country, particularly in Columbia, the scientists had listed him for future testing.

Then, as the remaining Whites underwent accelerated transformation and laboratory tests yielded no results—even if insignificant, biology and medicine experts turned their attention to Quinn.

There were few outcomes to hope for. Quinn was just one among other similar samples, and the experts feared he could turn Black at any moment.

Anticipating this moment, Quinn prepared to leave the house. The longer he stayed away from their hands, the safer his project would be. As a scarce White man, he needed to make himself scarce.

He paid the priest, who had become completely Black, a short visit at night.

"I'll call you when I'm free," Quinn told him. "It may take a long time, and you may not remember me. So just remember two words: Mercy Ray."

Waring didn't want to pry into Quinn's problems. They continued their conversation, and Quinn left home.

The next day, Quinn drove away in his car without knowing that a mob had set fire to the church. A pillar of black smoke rose in the sky, but he didn't turn around to see, nor did he look in the mirror.

Quinn's mind was preoccupied with deciding which neighborhood, or even county, to go to. He had already paid the rent on his house for the month in advance, and so the owner wouldn't know he had left.

Finally, he settled on the safest equation: the most racist place would be the friendliest for a White man in case he was discovered.

Hanahan, his destination, was so racist it was called Klanahan. But paradoxically, it was also known for being a friendly area.

All the way there, Black people stared at the White man. Perhaps they wished they were him. Or maybe they thought he was counting the hours before he would become like them.

It began to bother Quinn. Then he remembered that he was a runaway; an easily noticeable runaway. A white buffalo among a horde of black ones. He stopped the car at a side street, turned around to the backseat and pulled his bag.

He needed a shawl or a large piece of cloth to cover his face and big, black eyeglasses to hide the white areas around his eyes and gloves.

This was the least he could do to avoid drawing attention.

Without the hood of his jacket on his head, a completely covered head would make him look like a criminal or a looter. He found what he needed except for the cloth. Nothing was easier than tearing a shirt and using its larger piece.

Driving in disguise now became a comfortable ride. Also amusing. Twenty easy minutes took him there.

Before reaching the intersection of North Rhett Avenue with Tanner Ford Boulevard, a crowd of cars before the traffic lights slowed him down. Strange enough for the curfew state. Was it a temporary checkpoint to get him? Or it was just the usual bad habits of the divers here?

As he approached the queue of cars, Quinn noticed there were fewer vehicles than he expected. They stopped or slowed down a long distance before reaching the traffic signals. Police vehicles were parked on the right side of the road near a bank. Not an ambush, then, but an accident. A yellow ribbon fluttered in the air. The siren of a parked ambulance and its flashing lights. All around, including the police officers, were Black.

"What?!" Quinn shouted.

This was what he called a real surprise. A Black young man dangled, dead, from a tree on the right side of the road. A lynched Black. Two other Black men lay dead on the ground with the rope around their necks.

When closer to a police officer, he rolled down the passenger window and leaned toward him.

"Are they Blacks left from a cargo?" he asked the police officer.

"Drive away!" the officer ordered in a gruff, impatient voice.

Quinn pulled down the shirt from his white face.

"I'm just curious," he said.

The police officer's eyes shone with an emotion Quinn didn't miss. The officer opened his mouth with half a smile of surprise.

"Sorry, now, sir," he said, gently. "Now not a single Black animal is left. They're one-time Whites who hanged themselves."

"Ah, this one," Quinn said, still leaning forward. "Are people here beginning to commit suicide?"

"They are, sir," the officer answered.

"You'll see'em hanged hee-yah an' wherever ya drive. That's now if ya were faster than cops and ambulances. About a dozen in a single day."

"Too bad," Quinn said, not sure if he meant it.

"Keep your skin safe from the virus, sir," the police officer told him before Quinn covered his face and drove off.

The voice of the officer came far with a late question getting no answer, "How did ya escape the color change, sir?"

As the police officer had warned him, he came across another suicide scene on Tanner Ford Boulevard after two crossroads. A boy and a girl. Reporters were there. Maybe the same ones who had covered the lynching of Black men at the same place, Quinn guessed.

The calamity was explainable. The proudest Whites were the least able to cope with the transformation into Blacks.

As he drove on, the scene repeated itself; each time with slightly different details. Only one thing was missing: none of the dead were elderly. This, too, was explainable. The older people had fewer years to live and were less likely to be despondent.

Quinn no longer wished to stay in the area. He wanted to see the Whites suffer but not kill themselves. He was so bewildered he couldn't decide where to go. Confining himself in his Charleston's rented house was an option, but the worst. Going to Mount Pleasant was another.

He made his way back to try the latter, and drove on Interstate 526.

On Wando River Bridge, he could see the Cooper River Bridge, or Ravenel Bridge, on the right which not long ago, thousands of runners' feet of the short marathon thudded. All White feet and legs.

No Black runners and walkers, as they were in Gabon or waiting to be deported there, or lynched. Like the bridge he was now driving on, it was empty, save for a few passing vehicles and occasionally a police car operating its siren without meaning to arrest curfew breakers since most of them were armed and hostile.

Until he arrived at a hotel in Mount Pleasant he randomly picked, the scenes of young men's suicide grew fewer.

The receptionist raised her eyebrows in wonder on seeing a guest. Quinn feared she would ask him to show his face. She didn't. All the few other guests had their embarrassment covered.

She smiled. "In the end, all of us will hide ours. At least, outdoors," she said, without an introduction.

Quinn kept his answers brief, enough to let her know he had come for some business. He wondered how the hotel was able to stay open during the lockdown, but he didn't want to start a conversation.

He spent two uncomfortable days in the hotel before deciding on his next destination; an opener area.

His options were many. First, he thought of the beaches in the northeast. But they were too far. Then Isle of Palms and Sullivan's Island. Or retracing his steps, but on Cooper River, and head to the beaches of Folly Island and as far as Kiawah Island or even farther to Edisto Island.

Trying all or most of those places was another option. He began by spending two days in Isle of Palms; two enjoyable days since no tourists and only few locals were in sight.

Kayaking was a break for the brain. Then he went on a yacht tour to see dolphins after sunrise.

A now-Black family aboard were the only passengers with him. A mother and her two kids, and an old man, seemingly the grandfather of the kids, who was smiling as if frowning. The woman was relaxed, while the boy and his sister were worried that the dolphins would not be playful with them like they used to be with humans.

To their surprise, the dolphins approached and whistled. The two kids screamed with joy.

"The dolphins called us!" the boy shouted. "I was afraid they wouldn't."

"Why shouldn't they do?" the mother asked.

"Aren't we black?" the girl asked.

"It makes no difference for them," the mother said.

"How would you know?" the old man asked.

His question didn't surprise Quinn. He had expected the man to be racist.

"Blacks are human beings like us, Dad," the woman said.

The man looked the other way. The two boys were laughing and excited.

"God created both the dolphins and the humans, Dad," the woman went on. "The Whites and the Blacks and the Reds. Dolphins know this well."

A good woman and lovely animals and a bastard old man; Quinn thought about the family. And two boys, oblivious to the world. The old man was a seed of the devil.

This made him judge that another couple of days in Isle of Palms would be fine. But since it was now the Gypsies' strategy, he rejected the idea. Then he canceled Sullivan Island, too, for the sake of a longer ride.

Driving back to the peninsula and down to Folly Beach via James Island took him for two days of mandatory vacation. He spent another day there when he saw the people riding the waves on surfboards and seemingly not heeding their skin color change or the supposed epidemic. It was a place of medley, carefree people. This made him love to stay longer, but for now, he wanted a closer connection to nature. And Kiawah Island was that place.

Here like in other locations, he used a fake ID card. For each, he had a different one.

The receptionist, a short man with a few hairs on the front of his head, asked him to uncover his face. With a broad smile, the man told him he could pick any room he liked as the hotel was almost empty. Despite the change the receptionist had undergone like the others, he seemed to be retaining an inborn good mood.

"Who would ever love to enjoy his new skin color here?" the man said, still smiling. "It's shocking as all get out. Sunbathing became the last thing people want now."

Quinn nodded quickly as if laughing mutely at the unfunny joke.

And more sunbathing hours mean more guarantees for exposing oneself to Mercy Ray, Quinn thought.

The man went on. "But people don't think about the bright side of our misfortune. The skin's now black. The features are the same. Whites in blackface, like in a movie from the past. No bulged noses or inflated lips."

Quinn's hand instinctively rose toward his nose but he quickly lowered it, reminding himself that there were many white men with big noses and lips in the country.

This man's talkative, he thought. He'll tell everybody about a guest with a full mask.

The receptionist chattered so much that he forgot his request for the guest to uncover his face.

Then Quinn remembered that the receptionist was simply following the lovely old custom of Charlestonians who used to converse with people they didn't know. As racism ruined this and the other nice custom; waving for everyone they saw, Quinn encountered fewer such friendly people.

"The football game challenge to the lockdown is on TV today in Charleston," the receptionist said. "Don't miss it."

"I won't," Quinn replied.

"What's your favorite college football team?"

"Oh, none," Quinn answered. "Would anyone be interested in college teams?"

The man gaped at him for a moment.

"Well, I declare people here are breaking their old habits," he said as if talking to himself.

Once in his room, Quinn removed his mask and threw it away. He sat on the bed, stretched his legs, putting the right on the left, and rested his back against the headboard.

He picked up the remote control and switched on the TV, only to find that the previous guest had left it on Dorian Loyd's channel, The White Revival.

A Black correspondent was reporting in front of a building from which black smoke rose. Quinn recognized the voice as Zach's.

He sneered from the corner of his mouth.

"Proud White Zach is now shameful Black Zach," he said.

The report was about an attack on the building. The few minutes Zach spoke showed Quinn that the man wasn't feeling shame.

"He's still just as ardent and justifying racist crimes as he always has," he said.

Zack turned around to the building and said that it was burned for the third time. Quinn jerked in his bed. Reverend Waring stood opposite his burned church while four young men, three Blacks and one Brown, insulted him. A piece of the image of Black Christ lay near the door. Quinn wondered if the mob had destroyed everything in the church. There was something he had to check using his phone before watching the news.

When finished, the four young men were facing Zach. One grabbed him by the collar and shook him.

"What were you telling the people?" he asked him, frowning.

"Wait, wait. I'm Zach Martin from The White Revival channel," Zach yelled.

"He says he's Zach Martin," the Brown young man said to his friends.

"And who's Zach Martin?" the young man asked.

"I don't know," the Brown answered. "Maybe a VIPS."

"VIP," his friend corrected him.

"No, VIPS."

"And what's that?"

"A Very Important Piece of Shit," the Brown answered.

The young man continued shaking Zach.

"Whoever he is," he said. "He's asking the people to feel sorry for the church of the black devil."

Quinn enjoyed seeing Zach being humiliated while trying in vain to explain who he was.

The screen shifted to Joe, the anchor. White Joe's image was stamped on Quinn's brain. Now, Black Joe stunned him. Quinn stared at the screen for a few seconds before bursting into loud laughter.

He jumped to his feet, masked and left the room. On his way, he saw a few people biking on the endless beach. This was a place for nature to see and enjoy. And with small-sized structures compared to those on other beaches.

On his bike, he spotted loggerhead turtles coming ashore to lay eggs. It was early for the baby turtles to hatch and make their way down to the sea where they belonged.

Alligators were in every pond on the island, even going onto golf courses, and more frequently; on roads when they moved from one pond to another. Although it was their mating season and they were now active, the seashore here was safe.

In this place, where nature sharply manifested herself, Quinn felt freer. He wished he could stay there for the rest of his days before going back to where he belonged, but a new call for departure came from Columbia. John-Ward, the president of the Confederacy would give a speech to the State. Something important was going to happen. Something that might touch him personally.

CHAPTER 7

Quinn drove back to Charleston, opting for a hotel instead of his rented house. He switched on the mini TV to catch the news and the radio to listen to a Black station in Oakland, California.

The sounds of the havoc in the city coming through the live broadcast on The White Revival TV mingled with old Jazz music playing on the radio while the device on his car was relaying Mercy Ray ahead.

The TV showed people painting their porches, doors and everything in their houses with haint blue.

The news reporter explained it in the background, "It was 'haunt' that the Blacks called haint or ghost. An old tradition of Gullah-Geechee culture to ward away the spirits. It still exists in houses in Charleston, but the people here are reviving it everywhere as a theory beginning to spread about ghosts and evil spirits being the sources of the epidemic."

Joe Raymond appeared on the screen, leaning forward, pursing his lips, and frowning. "This is catastrophic," he said. "I mean, us seeking refuge in Negroes' beliefs. Let's see what catastrophe our reporter has to tell us."

The scene shifted to another area to broadcast chaotic reactions to the epidemic.

Young men and women were jumping down tall buildings. Men wrapped in swastika flags set fire to themselves.

Quinn judged they were the same people he had seen in White parades, but now with black faces. A young woman cried and bowed and put her hands on her knees among others her age; some who lay dead. Others kneeled and beat the ground with their foreheads.

Stop "killin' yourself!" the young woman cried, the jazz music from the radio overlaying her voice. "For God's sake, stop it!"

The camera turned to another side.

The music calmed down.

"Here comes another young lady," the reporter said. "She seems to be getting hold of herself."

The young woman leaned over a skinhead young man resting his forehead on the ground and crying.

A shower of rain fell. Quinn turned the wiper blades on.

"It's useless," she shouted. "It's over. All y'all are Black. Accept it as I did and live your life."

The music played louder.

The young man kept crying. Another raised his head to the woman and frowned at her.

"You seem to be Black since the day your bitch mother spat you," he shouted at her.

Stretching out his hand with the microphone, the reporter approached the young woman.

The music turned mild.

"Are you an original Black?" he asked her.

The young woman slapped his hand away.

"I'm whiter than you, bastard," she said between her clenched teeth.

The radio shifted to a quicker piece of jazz.

Joe Raymond spoke in the background, "We're going now to visit a calm area. Here's Zachary Martin in Morris Street in once a Black church the White folks put their hands on and rebuilt it. Some people came here to seek Jesus Christ's earthly salvation."

The rain stopped, but the wiper blades kept moving.

Two dozen men and women appeared on the screen, kneeling before a huge painting of Blond Christ. Some bowed their heads and the others rocked to and fro. All hummed prayers, asking Christ to come to their aid and recover their lost color.

Zach interviewed passersby outside the church.

"Did you think of going inside and asking for Christ's help?" he asked.

A saxophone squeaked.

"Christ won't help us," one answered. "He hisself wasn't White. Why should He care about us?"

Quinn turned the wiper blades off.

"We've lost everything," an old man said. "Our color. Our superiority. Even our chance for salvation. Jesus has turned His back on us and condemned us to Hell."

"But did we ever truly have the chance for salvation?" a woman spoke up. "We forgot that Black people were also created by God."

"Yes, Ma'am," the old man replied. "God created them. But God has His preferences."

"Preferences based on what? Skin color or actions?" the woman asked.

"Where's the president of the Confederacy?" another man asked. "Where are the government men? Why are the legislative guys hiding?"

Zach turned to face the camera.

A bass trombone played.

"That's the question on everyone's mind, Joe. The government is carrying on with its work, but only online. None of them have shown up. It's like a government of ghosts."

Raymond added, "We've tried to contact the government and the legislature, but aside from a handful who responded, all declined. They think it's some kind of virus and are afraid of catching it."

A tenor trombone joined in.

"Or they've already caught it and turned Black, so they're ashamed to be seen in public," Zach's voice came from the background.

"It's both, Zach. It's both," Raymond agreed.

A clarinet screamed.

"Those who caught the virus don't want to show up," he continued, "and those who are still healthy are afraid to interact with others."

Laughter could be heard in the background. Zach turned to see two Black teenagers approaching in a good mood.

A pickup truck tailgated Quinn's car. He drove in the right lane to let it pass. The driver passed, but then slowed down as South Carolinian drivers used to do.

The clarinet screamed again.

"Are you guys originally Black?" Zach called out.

"No, Broda," one answered, trying to speak in Geechee. "We binnuh White jes like snow an' now we black like coal."

"But you seem happy," Zach said.

"We wa ain dead, man," the teenager replied. "We wa ain dead an dat nuff."

"Stop speaking Gullah," his friend said. "They'll think we're really Negroes."

"Leh um tink so, Broda," the lad replied. "Dat ailment mek Black an' buckruh de same."

"Nobody is equal to any original Negro unless another Negro," Zach said.

"Aren't you precious?" the lad's friend said. "Why not bring back the white of your skin?"

"E ain able bring e white skin," the Geechee-speaking young man said. "De dog nyam um."

A jolly squeak of the clarinet.

Zach turned back to the camera, with a sad expression.

"Here's another aspect of our misery, Joe," he said. "Before long, we'll all be speaking Gullah."

The piano keys bounced with quick notes.

Quinn turned up the volume on the radio.

His car continued to spread its rays.

He managed to cover the entire Peninsula for one month, but he didn't know that a wolf hunt was about to be unleashed on him.

CHAPTER 8

Quinn was in his hotel room, listening to a voice message from Larry John-Ward, the president of the Confederacy. John-Ward gave a brief introduction on strength and solidarity before citing reports from medicine companies confirming the virus theory.

The companies were working tirelessly to find the cure and vaccine and needed more volunteers to test both infected and survivors. John-Ward called for an open-ended lockdown, although he couldn't impose it on the citizens. He begged them to understand the situation before it became more disastrous.

"There's a virus we know nothing about," he said. "It infected everyone. We need the lockdown to protect the few Whites and find out what spared them. It's also to prevent what would be more fearful than turning Black. That virus may alter everything in our bodies, from our features to our accent, and even our superior feelings and way of thinking."

The president's last warning only added to the public's panic. Hourly news about the progress of the medicine companies turned the once conspiracy theory into scientific fact. Initially, few volunteers were willing to take part in the tests, but living as a Black became equivalent to death, leading to more people volunteering.

The public began to suspect the intentions of the companies' owners, accusing them of hiding their white faces under black makeup. In response, the owners held a live event with other businessmen, washed their faces and hands, and allowed people to touch their skin, but nothing could stop the wave of panic.

The companies made a deal with the government to bring back some Black Americans from Gabon for testing. Despite the civil war in Gabon, an American mission of scientists and intelligence agents arrived at the area of influence belonging to the American-backed militia.

Knowing that the deal was vital to the mission's destroyed country, the militia demanded one million dollars for each person, whether an adult or a child.

The mission's offer was ten thousand dollars, which the militia refused. They deployed a force around the camp and shot in the air to disperse the Gabonese men and women who rushed to defend the Black Americans.

John-Ward agreed to pay one hundred thousand dollars, but the Blacks refused to go back home. He contacted the militia leader to force the cargo home; now for two hundred thousand dollars per capita. The militia entered the camp, killing and injuring those who resisted and selling the others as slaves.

On the day of their arrival, John-Ward addressed the Confederacy and announced the good news about the forthcoming, new medical research, and about a White survivor they were following, but who they had lost track of.

John-Ward urged the man to come forward and contact the authorities, as he was the greatest hope for the Whites. And at the same time, he offered a five million dollar prize for anyone who provided information about him.

The president ended his speech by requesting citizens once again to volunteer for the ongoing medical research.

The prize was the starting gun for a race to get the prey, but Quinn had fallen into a deep sleep and missed this last piece of the president's speech.

CHAPTER 9

After the president's address, what started as a wolf hunt quickly turned into a military campaign, with police forces and units of the National Guard fanning out across the city.

Groups of armed treasure seekers joined the chase, sometimes fighting amongst themselves in their quest for the prize.

The groups had little regard for the safety of the civilians caught in the crossfire. They believed that the last White man could be in every house and behind every door.

Quinn awoke to the sound of gunfire outside. He turned on the TV and saw a big fight going on. A clash between armed groups had erupted on the streets between Wraggborough and Radcliffeborough, with the hotel he was staying in located in the middle of the conflict.

The fight had started with an armed group entering the church of Waring after rumors about his links to White protesters.

Another group heard of them. Fearing their rivals would get away with the prize, the men rushed to the area, surrounded the church and called for their rivals to hand over the man.

Despite finding the church empty, save for the now Black priest, the first group was determined not to show their failure. They challenged the new group and a fight broke out. The resistance proved that the prey was inside the church, which only attracted more groups to the area and turned it into a battlefield.

Quinn became anxious about Waring. He reached for his phone on the stand beside the bed and looked at its dark screen.

Shutting the phone off after he left Charleston the last time had been a necessary precaution to prevent being tracked. Now, it was riskier to turn it back on.

He put the phone back on the stand, rested his head on his hands, and closed his eyes. Waring's image appeared to him for a few seconds, sad and tired. Quinn's eyes opened wide. Waring was worth the risk. After all, Quinn had done his job.

The only thing he feared was that if they could discover the secret of the ray, would they find a way to reverse its effect?

What if they did? They would forget everything and keep doing evil or even become eviler.

The past weeks had shown no signs of repentance whatsoever. Not even a single White supremacist had repented. They weren't ready to change their ways.

He picked up the cell phone again, and again looked at it.

"I'll take the risk for your sake, Julius," he said. "Whether or not you're still alive."

The phone rang. No response.

It became more worrying. But at least the phone was working.

Another try. And before the ringing stopped, Waring answered.

"Hey," Waring said.

"Waring!" Quinn said.

"Yes, sir?"

"It's me. You have my name in your contact list."

"Sorry, no."

"Waring, is it you? I mean Father Waring?" Quinn asked. He didn't have to. He was sure of the voice.

"Yes, I'm him. The application on my phone shows your name. It's … Mr. Peterson. How can I serve you, sir?"

"Father Waring! I'm Leo Quinn."

"Sorry, there was someone with that name I used to know. He died, and I attended his funeral. I don't know the other one."

"The other one?"

"Someone the police and the people and everybody are looking for."

Quinn swallowed hard. It was too late. He looked at the TV. The ribbon read: clashes continue between armed groups in Charleston to get Leo Quinn.

"Well," he said. "There are hundreds of Leo Quinns, maybe. I'm… I'm the guy… the Black guy who passed by your church and you hosted him for a couple of days because he had no money and… Mercy Ray."

"Mmm. I've hosted many people. Let me try to remember you. Well, I'm sorry, I don't recall. Maybe not the name, but

I'm sure I'd recognize your face. You said you're Black. Can you describe yourself for me?"

Quinn gave him a false description.

"I reckon I'm beginning to remember you now. Are you feeling better? And how did you manage to avoid deportation?"

Quinn fell silent for a moment, realizing he had made another mistake.

"Oh!" he said, his brain rotating like a mill to find an explanation.

There could be people monitoring the call. Then he remembered he hadn't mentioned the date.

"I was White when I passed by your church that day," he said at last. "I told you how miserable I was, how my family had abandoned me and all that. But now, everything's changed, and everyone became Black."

The two continued their conversation until they were sure they misled whoever was listening in.

But it was useless.

An intelligence agent monitoring Waring's calls found their conversation suspicious. He reported the call to his boss and gave him Quinn's location.

Feeling a sense of unease, Quinn jumped to his feet, packed his bag, and covered his face and eyes. He opened the door to leave the room, when someone came to his mind:

"Ella!" he exclaimed. "She'll be an easier target."

To warn her, he took his phone out of his pocket and looked at it.

"She needs to hide or go somewhere or even leave the country," he said to himself.

But making one phone call could lead the authorities right to her. He inserted the phone back into his pocket and chose the lesser evil.

Quinn left the room, unable to erase his traces. He left behind hair, skin cells, and other materials enough for the wolf hunters to find his DNA.

It was only a matter of time before they could get him. He needed to prolong his freedom for a few days, or even hours.

CHAPTER 10

Before notifying the FBI field office in Columbia City, the FBI resident agency in Charleston went into immediate action.

It took their men three hours to get to the hotel.

The receptionist informed them that the guest had already left, and they went into the room to gather evidence. As they worked, the receptionist chattered away, mixing fact and fiction.

Eventually, the man found himself a guest of the FBI in their car, protesting in vain that he had told them everything he knew. An FBI officer clouted him on the jaw, and he stopped talking until they reached the office.

While a quick, advanced DNA test was underway, the hotel receptionist repeated everything he had said earlier, now without his usual cheerfulness.

The FBI investigators played voice samples of suspected men for him. None matched Quinn's.

After trying out two dozen samples, the receptionist said the guest seemed to be muffling his voice and almost whispering.

His accent was definitely African American, he assured them, but he was trying to conceal it. For not revealing this earlier and wasting their time, the receptionist received another blow on the jaw.

With his face in his hands to protect it from an expected clout, the receptionist added that their target knew nothing about college football teams in Charleston.

Although two unreliable pieces of information said by the kind of people the receptionist was, they led the investigators to narrow the search to originally Black men from outside the state.

The DNA test on Quinn confirmed their conclusion: he was actually a Black man named Vesey Hunter. He was a scientist who worked at NASA's Goldstone Deep Space Communications Complex in Barstow, California, and then mysteriously disappeared while returning from a work trip to Australia.

The surprise was that Leo Quinn was a real person, another NASA expert, but an Australian who worked at a different part of NASA's Deep Space Network near Canberra. They worked together after NASA lent Hunter for six months.

Upon his return to the US, Hunter stole Quinn's ID information and used fake papers. Hunter had complained about racial discrimination at the Barstow station and during his temporary work. But despite sufficient evidence, NASA rejected his claims.

Fake Quinn left the FBI Resident Agency in Charleston and the Field Office in Columbia stumped, with the latter only partially informed.

Initially, both offices had wanted to run tests on Quinn to find out how he was able to remain untransformed. But it turned out to be the reverse; a Black man had transformed into a White man.

The Columbia Field Office questioned why Hunter had faked his identity, while Charleston office considered the question less important than the transformation itself. Some in the Columbia office suggested a possible connection between the two questions, and that the first could explain the second.

A greater surprise came on the next day. The FBI headquarters in Washington discovered that the real Leo Quinn had transformed into a Black after Hunter's return to America. All four of them, including Hunter, had been office mates at Canberra's Complex. Hunter had used some kind of virus or drug to change his skin color and his colleagues'.

Delving into Hunter's deep history revealed that his slave ancestors had lived in Charleston long before their descendants fled westward during the Great Migration. They had wandered until they settled in California. That was the only amount of information the FBI needed.

Quinn knew the rest. His ancestors had toiled in miserable conditions on rice plantations. It all started sometime after 1685 when a ship captain gave a quantity of rice seeds from Madagascar to two newfound friends in Charles Town in return for the kindness the town's people showed. Rice, or Carolina Gold, as Carolinians called it, brought misery to Africans even before the famous boom of cotton that did nothing but add to their suffering.

As the hoped-for savior of the country, South Carolina FBI used the name "The Last Hope" for their operation to capture the greatest threat on the country during the last five centuries. However, the FBI agents used another name among themselves: "Hunting the Hunter."

Expecting his foes to have discovered everything about him, Quinn kept only one item in his strategy: staying away from their hands for the longest possible time.

And to stay safe from their trap, Quinn planned to go somewhere he had never been before, firstly to states outside the Confederacy, although it was a long, dangerous way. Or maybe to join his wife, Ella; not in the little Barstow but in a big city. Ella and the baby— if it was born.

To track Ella on the web or by any other means to check on her meant letting his enemies track him.

But even outside the Confederacy, Quinn's freedom was at risk. He became the prey of everybody and every authority: supporters of the Confederacy, the federal government, drug companies, businessmen of all kind, and even foreign spies. He was worth more than the treasures in Ali Baba's Cave. Quinn was now the genie in the lamp who could shift castles from their places in a blink of an eye.

Roaming the city gave him no idea of where to go. His car was a good target, but a curious cab or carriage driver was equally dangerous. A little spot of his face showing from behind the glasses or mask was enough to take him to the nearest police station. When riding this or that vehicle, he hunched down in his seat as if mutely lamenting his bad luck like the others.

He longed for the bustling crowds of one of the many festivals in the city, hoping to disappear in the chaos. But every event had been canceled: the two-day Charleston Food Truck Festival, the Spoleto Festival and its little brother, the Piccolo Spoleto.

The Charleston Carifest had been canceled long ago, even when Blacks still lived in the city.

For three days, he wandered the city, his mind consumed with thoughts of finding a spot far away from the crime scene. And then he found it. After becoming the FBI's most wanted, no one would expect him to return to his starting point.

He made his way back to the Radcliffeborough neighborhood and spent the night in Marion Square.

Every hotel had become a trap. Otherwise, he loved to spend even one day in the Citadel.

Despite spring being the peak season for tourists, the hotel had offered a massive discount due to the loss of tourism.

And for Quinn, it felt like a good omen. But a better omen was Francis Marion's name.

However, the lockdown the people observed here —but only partially in every area of the city— made him stand out, even among the trees. A fox trapped in a cage in a square named after the Swamp Fox, the hero officer of the revolutionary guerrilla warfare against the British.

Marion's statue was missing and, instead, the city had reinstalled the statue of Calhoun and Hampton Obelisk after anti-racist protests removed them.

The Holocaust memorial remained but had been vandalized more than once, despite its obscure design that was neither striking nor referenced any Jewish symbol: only a vague shape of a curled carpet.

Insults were scrawled on the plaque. Swastikas and other White supremacist symbols were on the floor. Before the genes-hurricane, there had been a debate about what should replace it.

Quinn's first hour in the square proved that his good omen was a false one, and it turned out to be a jinx. And that was how it ended up.

A new morning brought wailing of police sirens. Quinn curled up on the grass, stretching one arm over his head. Footsteps approached, then the crackling of rifles. He sensed gun barrels pointing at him.

"Git up to yo feet," a harsh voice ordered.

Sitting up, he saw a police officer raise his rifle to shoulder level and close one eye.

Another officer, seemingly his senior, placed a hand on its barrel and lowered the rifle.

"Bless your heart!" he told his subordinate. "One bullet by accident is gonna destroy the nation. And sho nuff, our five-million prize."

Only then did Quinn realize the absurdity of the situation. The White police officers of yesterday, who had hunted and killed Black people, were now Black officers hunting a White man. He sensed that the senior officer was struggling to hide his Black accent. Mercy Ray had surely affected him deeply.

"I'm dying' to see his face," another police officers said.

"Y'all are gonna see it," the senior officer said. "Take off yo mask, bro."

For Quinn, removing the mask might have been the only good thing to get rid of what he felt was a shroud. Slowly, he unwrapped the shirt from around his head. On seeing the white face, the police officers whistled and wowed. The few bystanders who had come to the scene at the sound of sirens shouted with excitement.

Those were Quinn's last hope. He turned to them.

"They'll take me to their laboratories," he warned them. "They'll take every drop of my blood and say they couldn't find the secret of my staying White. And you will lose your last chance of becoming White again."

The men muttered between themselves, talking more about the prize than the man's warning. With pistols in their hands turned to the ground, a row of them moved toward the police officers. The senior police officer raised his rifle to his shoulder.

"Git back, y'all," he warned.

With one swift move, the men raised their arms and pointed their pistols at the policemen's faces.

A newly arriving cluster of men followed the row. The police officers moved backward, aiming their guns at the barrage of bodies. The men behind the armed row darted to snatch the weapons from the policemen.

"Git into the cars," the senior police officer shouted to his men.

In a matter of seconds, they got into their vehicles and sped away from the park.

The cars stopped at the corner of Tobacco Street and King Street, a safe hundred yards from the little crowd. Then feeling safer, they got out and waited for an opportunity to go back and take their prize.

The scene left Quinn stunned. Police officers everywhere used to shoot Blacks in situations less challenging than this one. The attackers were now Blacks. At least, the policemen saw black skins and this was enough for their subconscious to act as if they still were Whites, not transformed.

Quinn couldn't believe that the mentality of the police, notorious for their brutal behavior against the Blacks, had changed just because of a change in skin color.

A tough hand pulling Quinn's arm interrupted his thoughts. Four men encircled him. Then the group who attacked the police officers rushed back from their task.

"He's our man," one of them shouted.

"Then try to get'm," the one who was grabbing Quinn by the arm shouted back and then dragged him. Another one pulled him by the other arm. Two young of the group of four kept behind to stop the approaching group.

A huge man butted one them on the forehead and knocked him down. The other young man fled to join his friends.

A fierce brawl followed. Quinn fell to his knees and covered his head with both hands.

The huge man caught him from behind by the armpits and dragged him. Three youngsters joined the fight and kicked the man's back. They were about to snatch Quinn from him when a car rushed into the crowd, mowing down the nearest ones.

The others jumped to the sides. Making circles around the men, the driver hit anyone in his way.

Quinn rose unsteadily to his feet, swaying and bowing as he struggled to regain his balance. The car approached and abruptly halted, causing him to collide with its side and fall onto the front hood.

The door swung open and a masked man emerged. He embraced Quinn from behind and swiftly pulled him toward the passenger seat. Whoever the newcomer was, he was a better kidnapper for Quinn who leaned back against the seat with his eyes rolling.

As it resumed its meandering rush through the angry crowd, the car collided with other men as it made its way toward the edge of the square.

The burly man gave chase, leaped onto the back hood and tried to keep his balance on the zigzagging vehicle, only to fall and roll onto the ground.

With a dozen others in pursuit, the car made a full circle before finally exiting onto Calhoun Street. It turned left toward the first crossroad.

"I'm not gonna play with them till the cows come home," the driver said.

Turning right onto Meeting Street, the car rushed until it reached the street intersection with Burns lane, then with George Street, and Society Street, then with Wentworth Street. A half turn right, still on Meeting Street, and another intersection with Hasell Street, and more crossroads. Sirens of police vehicles blared from nowhere.

Quinn turned to the Black, masked man.

"If you continue driving as if drawing a straight line on a piece of paper, we'll end up on Broad Street and its Four Corners of Law, where we'll encounter more people and cars," he said. "Unless my hunch is incorrect."

"And which is?" the man asked.

"That you don't want to share the prize with anybody."

The driver braked after passing Hayne Street. "You're right about the first part," he said.

Quinn bowed, with his head spinning and his stomach churning.

"Are you okay?" the man asked him.

"Motion sickness," Quinn muttered, retching. "What about the second part?"

"Take this," the man said, throwing a shirt at Quinn. "It's to cover your face, not to throw up in it. I want no prize."

"If you're taking me to the police department, you could've let those behind take me and saved me this torture," Quinn said.

"I'm not carrying you to any police department," the man said.

Quinn noticed the man attempting to alter his voice. The car jerked forward. Quinn took his head out of the window and vomited, then wiped his mouth with his sleeve once he finished.

"Sorry," he muttered. "Some of it got on the back door."

"Never mind. Just cover your dangerous white face."

Quinn wrapped the shirt around his head and rested his back against the seat. Police sirens still echoed.

"Then to the FBI office?" he asked, gasping for air.

"Not even the FBI," the man said, now slowing down.

Quinn turned to him, surprised by the man saying "FBI." The citizens of the Confederacy typically dropped the word "Federal" from their vocabulary. Even the FBI officers referred to themselves as "BI." Some used "CBI" to denote the Confederacy and make the Union men mistake it for Charleston.

The man went on, "You'll stay with me in a safe place."

Quinn lowered his head in contemplation. He thought he recognized the voice. He glanced sideways at his mysterious companion who pulled down his mask with a slow and deliberate movement, revealing Father Waring's face.

"No wonder," Quinn said. "It's you."

Waring wore the mask again and moved his thumb backward.

"I'm now Waring the criminal," he said, smiling from behind the mask.

"That's why I failed to recognize you earlier," Quinn said. "But they deserved it."

As they approached the intersection of Meeting Street with Horlbeck Alley on the right and Cumberland Street on the left, Waring pointed ahead with his right forearm on the wheel.

"So, from here, which one do you choose? Caesar or Jesus?" he asked.

"I've always avoided the bustle of King Street, the Earthly Realm," Quinn answered. "Go to Church Street."

"You got this one," Waring said. "But not what Country Captain was."

"I've sampled Charleston's food, but not all of it," Quinn said. "I didn't come to the city to eat."

"I understand," Waring said. "You came to devour the city and so you explored every street."

"And every alley," Quinn added.

Turning left onto Cumberland Street and then right onto Church Street, Waring eventually stopped the car under the cover of trees. "We'll leave the car here and walk," he said.

The police cars were still wailing in the distance.

Quinn got out. "I suggest we take a palmetto carriage," he said. "It'll be a nice way to enjoy the city without the hassle of car sickness."

"Sounds like a good idea," Waring said. "Of course if we can find one in this curfew state. After all, we need to leave this car behind, as it's being tracked."

"And then they'll find it and track you."

"Not me," Waring replied, holding his hands up. "Just some poor fellow who was unlucky enough to have his car stolen. God forgive me."

They crossed through the area and entered Philadelphia Alley.

"Narrow paths like this one would provide us with better cover," Waring said.

"Uh, it's old Duelers' Alley," Quinn said. "Let's play it."

He ran on the cobblestone street and then turned around. They stood facing.

Quinn stretched his arm with an imaginary pistol.

"I understand that you came to rescue me," he said, closing an eye as if about to shoot. "And I can guess why. But how did you know about my trouble in the park?"

Waring raised his invisible pistol. "A woman in the square suspected you," he said, squinting both eyes. "You know that women notice social details more than us."

"And she told you to come and get the prize?" Quinn inquired.

"And then to share it with her?" Waring asked. "No, not that. An angel in the police department urged me to rescue you."

He shot a bang. Quinn put a hand on his heart and leaned back on his left side.

"I'll haunt this alley like the dead duelers of the past," Quinn said, pretending to be in pain. "You'll find my ghost next time you come."

They both laughed, and Quinn turned to run. Waring chased after him.

"An angel, eh?" Quinn asked. "And in a police department?"

"Priests don't deal with demons, you know," Waring said.

"And did the angel suggest the next safe hiding place for me?"

"Not him, but me," Waring replied. "My church."

"Your church?" Quinn asked, coming to a stop and turning to face Waring. "The one they hate and may attack for the hundredth time?"

"They'll see only the rooms visible to them. And only me as I sent my tiny staff home for their own safety," Waring said. "Hey Californian guy! I could overlook your mixing pineapples put on the kitchen counter with a pineapple in the guest's bedroom, but not mixing up Charleston's popular dishes."

"I know that pineapple is the symbol of hospitality in your hospitable city," Quinn said.

"And also a way to tell the guests to leave when you put it at the foot of their bed," Waring said smiling. "Again, you won't see any in your hidden bedroom. Never. Unless you choose to leave."

"Should we hide somewhere until the police vehicles stop wailing?" Quinn asked. "Maybe go to a museum?"

"Back to Meeting Street?" Waring suggested. "There are plenty of museums within a mile of there."

"Right," Quinn said. "Like the one we passed at the intersection with Market Street. A museum for the Confederates and their predecessors who enslaved Blacks. The one over there is Old Slave Mart for Blacks who were enslaved by the Confederates and their predecessors."

They were now standing on Queen Street, opposite the parking lot.

"I found this fact in books, not in a museum," Quinn went on. "The Whites changed many things to polish their history and show how kindhearted they were. Will we go for the last time if not shut down because of the lockdown? I've been there no less than five times."

"You five times," Waring said. "Me, ten. Five to remember African American slaves sold in auctions and five for my ancestors who have no museum for their memorial."

"What?!" Quinn exclaimed.

"Haven't I told you I'm Irish?" Waring said.

"I guess so."

"And a far descendant of one of those White indentured servants, mostly Irish, who lived a little bit better than Black slaves."

"This's new," Quinn said, grabbing Waring's arm.

"For your ancestors' sake, I won't go again," Quinn continued. "Why bother with lies?"

They turned right.

"Speaking about lies," Waring said, "did I tell you I used to be a racist priest?"

Quinn stopped and covered his head with both hands. "Oh no, man. I thought I was the one with surprises."

"Yes, I used to be," Waring said. "My Christ was the blond one with blue eyes. But I knew he was actually a man of color. I couldn't keep lying to myself. The Son of God was a man of color. I had to quit one of the two. Quitting my belief in him as the son of God was more endurable than the other way. Then gradually I began to love my colored Christ and hate racism."

They walked, Quinn following Waring. "God's will prevails," Quinn said.

They turned left onto Church Street, passed the crossroads of Broad Street, and continued their way on Church Street. Then they took another left to go onto Elliot Street and then a right onto East Bay Street. They passed Rainbow Row before choosing Tradd Street instead, as East Bay Street was too long.

Then Church Street again and they wound through the buildings until reaching Water Street, where the trees continued to cover their path.

The sirens started up again, but from a distance. Waring told Quinn to quickly cross the street and continue their meandering journey on foot in High Battery neighborhood. Quinn did; one time at ease, another treading and at times taking quick steps backward.

Strolling down East Battery Street with the waterfront on their left was their next choice.

Sirens ceased.

Quinn swiftly climbed the steps to the walkway while Waring continued down the street.

"You'll be an easy target for eyes," Waring warned.

"It's worth it," Quinn replied. "A closer view of the water helps me recover from motion sickness and the kicks I received in the square. Hey look! Here's the island that should've made Charlestonians think twice before working for the New Confederacy."

Fort Sumter showed in the distance in the sea.

"I should've put my device there and fired my first cannonball from it," he said.

They passed by The Battery and went across the street to White Point Garden. Here, like everywhere in the city, there were few people around, all Black, who had broken the curfew. They had come out and tried to enjoy their time, although none of them appeared to be enjoying themselves. The only ones at ease were Quinn and Waring, who entertained themselves with everything in the park.

The monument of Moultrie, a hero of the Independence War, stood without anyone close to it. A few people stood before the Confederate memorials. Quinn thought they should have done the opposite, given that the new Confederate leaders brought a second catastrophe to the city. Because of those leaders trying to bring back that history to life, Quinn beat all the southern states. He was an invader while the memory of Major General Moultrie was their savior.

Spotting a palmetto carriage, Waring elbowed Quinn, who was absorbed in historical comparison.

"Here's a carriage," Waring said. "A careless fellow about the curfew and the disease. And only one passenger, equally careless."

They followed the carriage and hopped in. Waring relaxed in his seat, crossed his fingers on his lap and began a hymn. Quinn listened. Waring reached the end and Quinn knew it was Psalm 151:

"My brothers were handsome and tall,

But the LORD was not pleased with them.

I went out to meet the Philistine,

And he cursed me by his idols.

But I drew his own sword;

I beheaded him, and took away disgrace from the people of Israel."

Looking out of the carriage, Quinn saw the few people on the streets. Black men and women were everywhere. And Black kids. This was funny. And also a subject to ponder over how those newly Black children were thinking of themselves and their change. With closed eyes, he rested his back on the seat.

Waring's calm iteration of the psalm came to his ears. Quinn whistled it in a low voice. The Israeli Goliath had left Palestine decades ago when the other Goliath; the White monster of racism, let him down to his enemies.

It was now the turn of this White Goliath. Quinn crossed his arms on his chest.

"And I've beaten him with his own sword," he said, continuing then to whistle the psalm as the carriage rumbled through the quiet streets of Charleston.

CHAPTER 11

Quinn spent three weeks within the confines of Waring's demolished church. He made a quick physical recovery in the first few days, but the second week weighed heavily on his nerves. Being trapped was nothing new to him; he had predicted worse.

Here in the church or in his home or anywhere else, he would have to endure hiding; at least when always covering his face. But expectations and knowledge didn't necessarily mean relief.

During his time in the church, Quinn began to understand Waring's religious philosophy better. Waring traced back the roots of monotheism in the early period of Christianity. It was a religion free from the complexities that religious sects had invented. Christianity in its earliest form consisted of three figures: God, the son of Man, and the believers. Jesus was a human being just like any other prophet and the son of Mary, the pure and virgin, and nothing more.

Later, the notion of the Son of God was created to compete with the religions of the pagans, especially the Romans, and to present a kind of religion the pagans were familiar with. The Romans held superior power, persecuted Christians, and considered them inferior.

This all made sense to Quinn, but the next step required more thought.

Waring believed that the creed of the Son of God led to another one: the children of God. Christ should have dominated over the Roman deities and the sons and daughters of those deities. Those who accepted Christ as their savior should have dominated the pagans. The latter were Satan's children, and therefore the former should have been the children of God.

So it began with a privileged man at the top, then privileged followers, and eventually, after a long time, a select group of followers, the Whites. The Black Man could never be a child of God. Besides, every Black the Whites knew was a pagan. But the white racists were unaware that black Ethiopia had adopted Christianity when white Europe was still steeped in paganism.

Although not settling on this conclusion, Quinn liked the simplicity of Waring's church. He hated the idea of someone being the son of God while he, himself, was just an ordinary man. As a strong and confident Black, he never treated his situation as a Black with bitterness.

Despite his fears, especially for Waring and Ella, he wanted to learn more about religion. He came to the conclusion that theology had destroyed every religion. With many original sources lost and the remaining ones raising many doubts and few facts, theologians felt free to invent new documented religions on the ruins of the old ones. He found that even Islam, with its richly documented sources, was not immune to this fate, as theologians had complicated its simple creed by speaking about trivial matters and considering them of top importance.

As Quinn continued reading, he learned that there was a time when people thought of getting rid of religion and its sects in the public domain to bring peace to the world. However, the secularism that replaced religion turned out to be more brutal and disastrous. It was a new religion; an earthly one. It preached the equality of human beings but ended up creating the concept of superiority; one example of which was the super race. Racism, as a deviation from Judaism, Christianity, and Islam, was a product of secularism.

Even in liberal countries, the super race manifested itself in the notion of democracy that was suitable for the White Man but not for others. This theory was declared in the nineteenth century and was practiced in the twelfth and twenty-first centuries. Western democratic countries aborted democracy in other nations when their interests were at risk. Liberalism wasn't necessarily against racism, at least when it tried to impose its values on other nations as universal.

"Not only had man invented weapons of physical mass destruction, but also weapons of mental destruction."

That was Quinn's conclusion. And so, he made up his mind about the protective alloy he had invented. Mercy Ray was his mass destruction weapon, but he used it to teach a lesson to those who lived in hypocrisy.

"I'll destroy the alloy and its secret," he told Waring.

If this had been in the past, Waring would have tried to convince his friend not to do it in the name of God, humanity, or whatever would benefit. But now, Waring couldn't even discuss it with Quinn. The three weeks had passed, and there were no signs of the one-time Whites repenting, except for a few brave and religious or humane individuals. Waring thought the majority would become more savage if they regained their skin color.

Quinn needed fresh air for his brain before his lungs needed it. Loyd's TV channel announced a speech by the group's leader for his followers in Hampton Park at 3 p.m. Seeing the now-black leader live was more enjoyable than watching him on TV, and it was even better to see the distress of his now-black fans. Quinn felt a sense of double pleasure: fresh air and fun.

CHAPTER 12

Loyd paid a visit to Ashley, his soon-to-be-ex-wife. She opened the door, looked down, then let him in without a word. With slow, but resolute, steps, he followed her. He stood facing her in the living room, crossing his hands on his belly. She looked at him with stern eyes, but he stood her stare.

"Although now Black," he said, "you're still as pretty as a peach."

He chuckled briefly.

"How funny that we, the sacred White family, became inferior Negroes," he remarked.

Ashley remained silent, staring him down.

"But I find it hard to call you a Negro," Loyd added, clearing his throat.

She wanted to tell him she loved to call him a Negro. She thought he deserved it .

"If you've come to ask me to go back with you," Ashley finally spoke up, "then—"

Loyd interrupted her with a slow hand gesture.

"No," he said. "Not for that. I just came to say sorry. I would've asked you to take me back if it would've done any good. But it won't. It's over now."

They locked eyes for a moment longer before Loyd lowered his head and turned away. Without another word, he left, forgetting to close the door behind him.

Ashley turned on the TV and scrolled through the channels until she found Loyd's channel. She thought it was wise she didn't delete the channel. She could now listen to his lies for the last time before deleting it.

Quinn left early to stroll around the area and observe the effect of Mercy Ray on a new day before attending the speech. The cloudy sky promised a lovely shower, marking the end of spring.

Every place in the city was less crowded than usual. Commercial areas, shopping streets, and sports centers that were usually busy at that hour were almost empty.

He took a longer route starting from King Street to enjoy something he rarely had time for: looking at the many restaurants to pick one and have lunch. Although not so much interested in food, Charleston's delicious food made him gain two pounds. But he realized that it wasn't the right time for this idea, so he put his hand on his belly and told it to forget it.

Quinn noticed the increased number of people, mostly young, covering their faces. They either wore white gloves or pushed their hands into their pockets. Every woman wore trousers or heel-length skirts, or long socks if the skirts were shorter.

In addition to their mental torture due to their skin color change, they had to endure the heat and humidity while wearing too much clothing. On the positive side, this meant an end to the torture of bugs, eliminating the need for sprays they used tons of them in the past.

Maybe the worst were the "No-see-ums" that bit without warning. Quinn's satellite was another kind of No-see-ums: it was tiny, mentally and socially painful, and biting without warning. And no clothes or spray could stop it.

A brief shower interrupted his thoughts. A group of middle-aged men appeared from the street corner. With their heads covered and wearing flags of the Confederacy or the State over shirts with The Palmetto Regiment's logo, they walked with tense posture in front of him. He moved faster to leave them behind. Their conversation showed their destination was Hampton Park .

Before the endless street ended, he turned left to leave it and move into the areas. And then the crosswalk bridge on Sheppard Street and US 17, that here and elsewhere in the Peninsula was once called Septima Clark Parkway (after the black activist woman), or the Crosstown (its old local name, officially reused of late). Then across Mitchell Playground to Rutledge Avenue. Half a mile brought him to Hampton Park .

He had heard of the monument of Denmark Vesey in the park. As expected, the statue of the Black alleged rebel was missing and replaced with a monument of Robert Hayne, a slaveholder and the state Attorney General when Vesey was hanged.

In the park, less than a quarter of Loyd's usual audience gathered. The few people arriving at short intervals wouldn't add much. The rest of his fans preferred to stay home and watch him on TV. More than half of the attendees covered their faces. No one was yelling or cheering. Some were ready to weep as soon as their leader's speech would start.

A procession of white cars came along Jenkins Avenue and stopped at the intersection with Mary Murray Drive. Loyd got out with his men and walked among the few people in the trees. He moved to the duck pond, around which more people gathered. Some wept on seeing their leader black before he could say a word.

Loyd stopped before the bridge. The four men following him stopped behind. He stood in the middle of the circle, looked ahead for a while and turned around to the men.

"Will you please stay with the people," he told them. "Tom, come with me."

Schultz, his deputy, followed him with a little leather bag in his hand.

The clouds rumbled.

A stall, with a microphone on it, stood in the middle of the bridge that spanned the pond. Looking down, Loyd walked with heavy steps to the stall. He took the microphone, let it go, rested his hands on the stall, took the microphone again, and finally put his hands on the stall. All feeling sorry for themselves, the audience didn't notice his confusion except for Quinn, who also saw Loyd's hands slightly shaking.

Loyd looked out at the smallest audience he had ever seen gathered to hear him speak. But their number relieved him. A bitter smile appeared on his face.

The cloudy sky thundered again .

"I understand why the others haven't come," he began his sermon, "as they were all once brave men and women and still are. However, we're faced with a situation that even the bravest among us struggle to confront. It's blowing up our sense of superiority. It's akin to Jesus Christ discovering He was the son of Satan, not God. And it's like the citizens of Charleston awakening one day to realize that their city wasn't the Holy City, but a cave hiding every wicked spirit."

Loyd's rhetoric not impressing him, Quinn pouted. "But you still haven't realized that you were and still are the son of Satan or one of those wicked spirits," he said in a low voice .

The closest one to him, a young man, turned with disapproval in his eyes. But he didn't comment.

Loyd went on, "One day, all felt the bitterness of being marginalized for the sake of Blacks, Reds and Yellows. Asians, Jews and Muslims. Then came our hero; the president who revived the glory of the White race. And when we were about to drink the wine of our victory, we woke up to see ourselves Negroes. Isn't it ironic that we're now Negroes gathering in a park our predecessors named after the man who owned the largest number of slaves? We kept the name during the heresy of what they called Black Civil Rights and till nowadays just like how we kept the names of the other slaveholders and other leaders alive: Wragg and his children, Middleton, Henry Hammond, Thomas Heyward Jr., John Ward, Aiken Jr., James Ladson, Senator Strom Thurmond and the rest of our heroes. But all are turning in their graves on seeing their blood running in the veins of Negroes."

With a bitter smile on his face, he shook his head. "And it's another irony that our state was the first to cede from the

Union in the past and we planned to do the same for its glory," he said. "But our state became the first to be kicked out from the superiority of the white color. We haven't even had the opportunity to enjoy the anniversary."

A few heavy seconds passed before he turned to Schultz and said, "My bag."

Tom stepped forward, gave him the little bag and retreated to his place. Loyd put the bag on the stall.

"I promised to find a rescue," he said to the audience. "But I found none."

He unzipped the bag, pushed a hand into it and looked at the people .

"I feel now I got the courage to admit that we've been defeated," he said. "We were one step from rescuing the white race, but the evil defeated us without giving us a chance to shoot a single bullet."

Quinn expected the next thing to take place. "This's how life goes, dude," he commented, again in a low voice. "Sometimes you lose at the last minute. And then you must shoot the bullet of farewell."

Loyd took his hand out of the bag with a pistol in it.

"Yet, I still don't admit my new color," he said. "We did nothing wrong. We didn't commit any sin to confess. We just acted according to the order of the world. Our project was the fulfillment of God's plans. I'm still a White man. A White, but in a false picture."

He looked at the sky. The men gaped. The women covered their mouth with both hands.

"And this wicked, false picture must be killed to let the good and real one come to life," he finished his words.

He raised the pistol with resolution and inserted it into his mouth. And before anyone could shout to stop him, he shot it.

Loyd fell backward into the water. Shrieks of horrified women followed the bang. Some men cried. Others knelt and bowed and wept. A light shower fell on the place.

Quinn pushed his hands into his jacket pockets and turned to leave. Shouting in panic, some men rushed toward the pond and jostled past Quinn, who no longer had the desire to witness another live misery.

Crossing his fingers, Schultz stayed on the bridge, watching as the water turned red and Loyd sprawled on his back.

The white of the water, the black of Loyd's face and hands and the red around his body made what seemed to Schultz the most striking contrast he had ever seen. He picked up the pistol, stepped aside from the rushing men, and left toward the trees.

Ashley watched the event until the last minute. Her husband's body in the red water meant nothing to her. He died the day he visited her in the hospital. She shut off the TV.

Amid the wave of terrified people, Quinn kept walking away with the idea of catching the rest of the story on television. Loyd's final words lingered in his mind, feeling like a familiar scene he had once witnessed in a film or novel.

He was racking his brain to recall the scene when the sound of another gunshot echoed in the distance, prompting him to stop to hear other gunshots. None followed. He guessed who the second was.

Retracing his steps through the same winding route would have distracted his thoughts. Instead, he needed to focus on outlining his plan for the upcoming days. His way back on Rutledge Avenue was straightforward and without any turns .

Lost in thought about the outline, he found the campus of the Medical University on his right before reaching Calhoun Street.

"Well," he mused to himself. "One leader had already perished before the university could identify the supposed virus. I can imagine the experts hunched over their devices, squinting, and sweating and can picture the teams' leaders running here and there to check the results. And all are saying, 'Nothing so far. It's frustrating.' And yes, it'll keep them frustrated."

As he attempted once again to recall the scene Loyd had referenced earlier, he found himself whistling Psalm 151.

CHAPTER 13

Finally, Quinn knew he should surrender. After setting a date, he told Waring that there was one last thing he should do. Waring didn't ask what it was, for nothing could be more harmful than what had already passed. But Quinn felt it was necessary to let him know. He revealed more about the ray and the satellite. Waring's mind accepted everything in Quinn's story except for the satellite's size.

"Are you telling me that the satellite you sent to space to overturn history is only nine cubic centimeters?" he asked. "How much is that in inches?"

"A little over half a cubic inch," Quinn replied. "About the size of eight sugar cubes - four on top, four on the bottom. I could've made it the size of one sugar cube, but NASA would've questioned the student who made it."

"NASA? Student?"

"We call it a femtosatellite. It's a very tiny satellite. I can't launch any satellite into space. NASA can. They have programs for students, and one of them was launching tiny satellites they made alongside other apparatuses. The White Australian student presented his failed satellite, and I replaced it with mine. I let it relay a radio wave to this place in our cruel world, but then I replaced it with the ray that my device broadcasted. And now I want to go to where my device hides and shift the ray to other parts of the country to make their people black. Only one slight movement of the antenna will change their history."

Waring sat down, facing his friend. "Do they deserve it?" he asked.

"They do. Many chose silence. Many others are but Copperheads. Keeping silent when others are treated with injustice is a partnership in the crime."

"Will you tell the people here about the ray?" Waring asked.

Quinn shrugged. "I don't know for now," he said. "Maybe. I may tell them the ray has a reverse effect, something I'm still not sure about. At least to make them migrate to the states outside the Confederacy and suffer from self-deportation like they deported the Blacks. They'll suffer more when those states refuse them. And how funny it'll be when they see the Blacks there turning white. They may weep and say, 'those Niggers stole our color.'"

Waring bowed his head and rested it on his balled-up hand. He stayed silent for a while. Quinn let him ponder over it without interrupting his thoughts or inspiring him with what to say.

"I understand your motives," Waring said at last. "I can't say it's unjust. We lost the right meaning of justice long before the Confederacy was formed."

He looked up at Quinn.

"I'll drive you to the place of the device if you want," he said.

"It isn't far from here," Quinn said, smiling. "I don't need a car. I don't even need to go out of this place."

Waring stared at his friend, who then walked out of the room. Waring stood up and followed him. Quinn stood at the top of the cellar stairs.

"Come with me," he told the priest. "After all, it's your place, not mine."

When they got to the cellar, Waring remembered the little box Quinn had asked him to keep there when he left his house on his journey. It was a broken case of an old-fashioned computer. Everything in the cellar was broken. The mob stole the valuable items and broke the trivial ones.

Quinn removed the case and showed the device. Even without the case, it wasn't worth stealing.

"The batteries need charging," Quinn said. "I'll plug the device into the power outlet, if you don't mind."

"I do mind," Waring said. "Not under the ceiling of my church, Leo… or, Vesey. It's not because I consider it a crime. I'm just afraid it'd be a sin against the non-Redeemers who are much more than we can imagine."

"I too am sorry for them," Quinn said. "But in the final account, it's a matter of philosophy of punishment. You're the kind of priest who prefers forgiveness even for sinners. My philosophy is different. It's that everyone is a sinner if he says it's none of his business when injustice is practiced against others, especially under the ceiling of a country they share."

"I tell you what, this makes sense," Waring said. "But I'm still not comfortable with finishing your project here. I'm a proud scalawag."

Quinn nodded. "And as a carpetbagger, I won't insist on you," he said. "It can work anywhere. And for less than one month. I'll rent another house and let the device stay there."

"Maybe you won't need to show your face to the householder," Waring said. "But everybody knows your name better than theirs. The householder will ask for your ID card."

Quinn smiled. "Yes, but then he'll read: Leo Quinn. But there are ID cards of Billy Andersen, Mark Rogers, Jack Austin or John Austin, I don't remember which one."

"One last question," Waring said. "Why did you call it Mercy Ray?"

A faint smile came to Quinn's face. "It's a mercy for the Whites," he answered. "Without it, their groups would've fought each other. You could've seen bloodshed all over Charleston and the Confederation when no more aliens to see. I don't know if political sociology mentions it or not, it's a social law that governs extreme armed groups. But those groups are now united in misery."

Quinn picked up the device and walked up the stairs, then outside the church.

"Come back when you finish your work," Waring called out after him. "I'm fixin' to cook crab rice for dinner. Do you like it? If you know what it is."

Quinn didn't answer, instead waving his hand as if to say it made no difference to him. Waring watched him cross the street and walk on the other side.

Waring sighed. "Farewell for now, my friend," he said to himself. "The will of God always wins. That's all I can use to explain everything happening."

CHAPTER 14

Quinn had finally completed his last job and was ready to bring the story to a close. He sat down for breakfast with Waring without engaging in any conversation.

There were a few small yet significant details left to attend to before heading to the FBI office. He carefully shaved his head, making sure his scalp was smooth like a bald man's. He then washed his head thoroughly to ensure no stray hairs remained. By going bald, Quinn wouldn't have to worry about FBI agents questioning him about wearing a wig. Applying powder to his scalp concealed any remaining hair roots. He donned the wig and wrapped his head with a cloth, leaving only his eyes visible behind big, black eyeglasses. He completed his disguise with black plastic gloves.

The two men hugged goodbye, both feeling the strangeness of the situation. A Black man who was now White and a White man who was now Black were united in their shared case.

"God created a man and a woman and told them that all their offspring will be and should be equal," Waring said. "Satan was the first creature who believed in a superior race. The children of Adam split into two parties: followers of Adam and followers of Satan."

Quinn asked, "Are we the followers of Adam?"

"I pray to God," Waring replied as he squeezed Quinn's arms.

"You should be going now," he said.

Quinn nodded and walked to the door, not looking back until he reached the street corner. Waring remained in the doorway, invisible to Quinn, who hailed a cab that took him close to the FBI office. He chose to walk the remaining half-mile to the building to savor a few moments of freedom before facing the unknown. Given that there was no chance of escaping on foot, there was no point in studying the building for a potential exit. The old office had been small, and he could have fought to the death for a slim chance of escape. The new building was larger and looked like a mini-castle.

He walked through the small yard leading to the office and took a deep breath, a smile spreading across his face.

"I did a great job," he said. "And one great job in one's life is enough to die like a hero."

When he reached the checkpoint, the guards asked him to remove his mask and the black eyeglasses.

"You can search me for weapons," he told the guards. "But if you want to know the secret behind the epidemic, you must allow me inside like this."

"I'll call an officer and you can tell him about the secret you claim you know," one said.

"I'm sure I know it," Quinn firmly said. "And no for telling any officer about it. My information is worth seeing Mr. Edwards, the Resident Agent in Charge, himself."

The guard whistled. "You want to see the boss!" he said. "Your information must be the name and nationality of the virus."

"Sort of," Quinn replied.

Another guard informed an officer inside that a masked man claiming to know the secret of the epidemic wanted to see the RAC. He added an explanation of his own: the man refused to remove his mask because he wanted the prize without anyone knowing his identity.

Two officers escorted Quinn inside to meet the RAC. Quinn sat down, and before revealing the nature of his information, he removed his gloves. On seeing his white hands, the men stared in shock. Then Quinn slowly pulled down his mask to reveal his white face. The sight of him stunned Edwards and the officers.

"I'm Leo Quinn. Or let me say, Vesey Hunter. The mysterious man you seek," Quinn announced, interrupting the tense silence in the room. All present shared surprised glances before quickly standing to their feet. Quinn remained seated.

Edwards' hand searched the table for the landline. An officer moved to it, dialed the telephone operator and held the handset up to his boss's ear.

"Call the President's hotline," Edwards said. "The President of the Confederacy."

"Shouldn't we contact the field office in Columbia?" one agent asked.

"No," Edwards replied firmly. "This guy's ours."

With the men not seeming to ask him questions at the moment, Quinn expected an upcoming interrogation party. He removed his wig.

"Will you please keep this here?" he told Edwards, handing him the wig. "It's the only wig I found to fit me."

As Edwards put the wig in a drawer, Quinn wondered if he would ever need it again.

Before nightfall, an army of interrogators, mostly scientists with two Charleston FBI agents and two from the Colombia office, surrounded him.

A questioning session, mixed with threats, lasted until a late hour of the night. Quinn's repeated answer was one sentence: he had inherited a gene mutation. He refused to provide any further details. Waiting to hear from him about the virus, the interrogators told him that he was lying.

A representative from a medicine company showed the toughest objection to Quinn's explanation. The interrogators understood his motives: the mutilation theory could make developing the vaccine —and hence gaining hundreds of billions of dollars— a much more complicated task, if not impossible.

A second questioning session began at six in the morning and lasted until noon without Quinn adding anything. In the afternoon, they changed their strategy. The medicine company representative suggested using torture. Except for one, the scientists agreed, but with the condition of keeping their last hope alive and able to speak.

Waterboarding was their first choice, but since it was so old-fashioned that Quinn might have known it wasn't lethal, they ordered a box to be ready as the last resort.

They tied Quinn to a bench, placed a cloth over his face, and poured water onto it. Quinn prepared to endure the sensation of drowning. Even if they immersed him in a pool, they wouldn't let him die, as he was worth a fortune.

After the first few seconds of water entering his windpipe, Quinn realized that waterboarding in books was a lovely mental picnic compared to the suffering he was experiencing. If he had any chance of being spared, he would have talked. But he knew they would hang him like a dog as soon as they got what they wanted.

"I won't die. I won't die," his brain repeated. "They need me. They'll stop it to keep me alive."

The end of the first shift brought relief, but only for a few minutes when the interrogators told him what was next.

"Something else everybody knows well, but this knowledge is equal to nothing," one scientist said. "Dogs won't kill, but bring men close to death."

For God's sake, what are they? Scientists or butchers? Quinn wondered.

He needed a minute to remember that he, himself, was a scientist who had transformed millions of people into Blacks.

"But they deserved it," he repeated his philosophy to himself, trying to find some relief. "Even those whose only fault was to believe it was none of their business."

A harsh barking came from outside the room. The scientists gave Quinn one last chance.

"Before you go under the mercy of the dog," one said, "tell us about Mercy Ray."

The two words stunned Quinn. He looked down.

They knew about it, he said to himself, and wondered how he should respond.

"Who's he?" the man asked.

Quinn's eyes widened as he looked up at him.

"Or she," another said.

Yes, she, Quinn thought, feeling relieved.

"I bet it's a pseudonym," the first scientist said while Quinn was wondering where they had heard the name.

"She's my wife," he answered.

"Ella Hunter," an FBI agent said. "Why would you call her Mercy Ray? A partner in spreading the virus?"

"She knows nothing," Quinn answered. "I wanted to protect her."

"But you're not alone," one of the scientists said. "Tell us about the others."

"No others," Quinn said.

"The priest," another said.

"What priest?"

"Julius Waring."

Quinn pretended to be thinking.

"No idea," he said.

He knew they would not believe him, but he bet on their possible lack of information.

The men shared glances. One nodded, then another spoke into his phone.

The door burst open. A huge brown police dog charged in with a man struggling to keep its leash five feet away from Quinn.

"You see that the dog may escape its leash at any moment," a scientist said.

"I see," Quinn said, trying to overcome his shivering voice. "The brown canines with which you tortured the brown men in Abu Ghraib and Bagram."

It was a history of the brown people he knew all too well. Only a few of the men remembered the two names.

With the possibility of the man failing to keep the collar in his hand, Quinn couldn't focus on the fact that his life was most valuable to these men. They wouldn't let the dog tear him apart, but they might let the dog take a bite if they grew tired of him. The harsh barking and sharp teeth, and the savage look in the dog's eyes froze his mind and muscles.

Staying motionless and staring at the dog made the men think he wasn't afraid. A man entered with a box in his hands, relieving him. Being shut up in a two-foot cube box was severe torture, but it was steady and without surprises like a dog's attack.

The other man took the dog out. Its barking faded away as Quinn found himself in the box. His body curled up, and his head went below his knees. He felt the last vertebra in his neck about to break. The worst part was his shortening breath. The men left the room. Quinn knew they would not come back that soon and that he underestimated that small object.

In the little cage, he thought of all the torture forms he now liked: electrical shocks, too noisy music, electronic noise, a guy raping him… and even that guy raping Ella, his wife, before his eyes… this one stormed his mind. A white curtain covered his eyes. Ella stood, laughing with joy and holding their baby. But those old days were never happy. Even with those he loved, life was a mixture of his struggle and the Whites despising him.

"But I revenged my nation. Yes. I revenged," his mind echoed before he fainted.

*   *   *   *   *

The Confederate States celebrated Quinn's capture. White groups and other people crowded in the cities and towns, dancing, cheering and setting off fireworks. John-Ward, the president, gave them the good news. His voice on the radio was broadcasted in the gathering places to joyful people who didn't ask why he still hid his face.

In Charleston's Gadsdenboro Park, the White groups had gathered, with The Palmetto Regiment leading the charge to take over the space. It installed a large screen to showcase cities of the Confederacy celebrating the event. The screen displayed photos and speeches of Dorian Loyd when White. And with every change of the scenes, the crowd cheered and waved their flags.

The screen then shifted to Washington D.C. Thousands of people stood before the White House, raising and waving flags representing the White groups, the Union, and the Confederacy.

Back in Gadsdenboro Park, the crowd cheered even louder. Then came an announcement over the speakers about a speech by Larry John-Ward, who was so glad he started without an introduction.

"We're only a few steps away from discovering the epidemic," the voice came, strong and confident. "We all will gain back our color before the year is over."

The crowd raised their fists in solidarity and cheered, chanting the Confederate anthem.

God save the South, God save the South,
Her altars and firesides, God save the South!

"We'll bring back the color of our country," John-Ward continued to speak. "The color of its glory and purity."

The crowd chanted:

Now that the war is nigh, now that we arm to die.
Chanting our battle cry, "Freedom or death!"
Chanting our battle cry, "Freedom or death!"

And as if he heard the anthem from his place, he raised his voice:

"Our ancestors chose between freedom and death. We too made the same choice and gained freedom. Our freedom from other races. And we'll be freed from this curse."

The throng boomed out in a fast rhythm:

"Freedom or death!"
"Freedom or death!"

As John-Ward finished his speech, the park thundered with all the anthems: The Palmetto Regiment's, The

Redshirt's, The White League's and the rest of the groups, Dixie, South Carolina's and the anthems of every state in the South.

*   *   *   *   *

Waring was embracing his knees and watching the TV channel that shifted from one city to another, showing what looked like a national feast.

In the FBI office, things were frustrating for the investigators, as Quinn continued to insist on silence, risking the leak of their failure. His death due to torture was another failure. To Quinn's relief, they made medical checks between torture sessions. Unable to send a word to the nation, his only hope was the mob growing impatient and some of them trying to attack the office.

The first signs of this public impatience began on the third day of celebrations. With no official giving announcements, rumors spread that the detained expert had destroyed every document relating to the virus. The fourth day was a day filled with grumbling and protests. Then another rumor turned their complaints into a frenzy. Website outlets spread news about the interrogators' links to the federal government, which planned to kidnap the man and find a cure before the Confederacy could do so.

At first, the Confederacy government ignored the news, but as the week of festivals went on, furious protesters marched to Charleston's FBI office. Protesters from other cities and towns in South Carolina traveled to join those surrounding the office. Soon after, waves of people from other states in the Confederacy joined in.

The president of the Confederacy refuted the conspiracy rumor and stressed that the remedy would be for all Americans.

With the herd mentality taking over the street, the protesters refused the logical explanation that later was answered by a third rumor. This time, members of the Confederacy Congress accused the federal government of planning to keep the Confederacy states Black and then deport its Black people there. This news was too much for the fretted people to bear.

A sea of frustrated crowds encircled the streets around the FBI office. A helicopter landed on the roof, delivering airborne troops and went up to allow another one to unload its soldiers. News spread that two helicopters had taken the man outside the building. On hearing the rumor, snipers positioned themselves on nearby buildings and waited for any other helicopters that might arrive.

The gathering people stayed in place even when intermittent shooting between the snipers and the force on the top of the office threatened to turn into a full-blown conflict.

Fresh news from outside the Confederacy shocked the entire country: Black newborns and white teens were transforming into Black in every state. The Federal government declared it an epidemic and imposed a lockdown. More cases among people who had been to Charleston and the South affirmed the conspiracy theory.

The crowd gathered outside the FBI office dismissed the news as a distraction from the federal government's operation. But as cases multiplied, their hysteria erupted. They launched an attack on the office. The Palmetto Regiment started the attack by climbing the fences.

The interrogators increased the pressure on Quinn, urging him to confess before the mob could breach the building. Four men kicked and hit Quinn as he bent over to protect his head. A final blow to his belly sent him crashing to the floor. The yells of the attackers grew louder and closer. Gunshots reverberated from all directions as if a gunfight had broken out in every room.

Two helicopters arrived and hovered to get ready for a landing. Halfway down, the snipers received them with bullets, killing one pilot. The helicopter spun out of control before crashing onto the edge of the roof of a nearby building, and then plummeting down onto the street below. The other helicopter's machine guns responded with salvos.

The mob broke into the building. Two FBI agents dragged Quinn toward the elevator. Edwards, the Resident Agent in Charge, the interrogators, and the scientists followed. They reached the roof and contacted the pilot. Before the pilot could warn them, the snipers killed three of them. The rest fell to the ground, and the helicopter supported them by unleashing rounds from its machine guns. It descended further, but a newly arriving group of attackers showered it with machine-gun fire.

With the situation on the ground worsening, the helicopter received orders to withdraw. The mob cheered their victory. Carl Dylann, the leader of The Palmetto Regiment's armed brigades, led the first group to the floor. His militiamen shot the FBI agents and scientists, lifting then Quinn on their shoulders. Edwards jumped to his feet and tried to follow them. Dylann struck him on the chest with the butt of his gun, and he fell to one knee. Dylann leaned over the parapet, facing the yard, and shared the good news with the people below. They cheered at the top of their voice.

Quinn stretched his hand towards Edwards, who approached, frowning with pain and placing a hand on his chest.

"Get me my wig," Quinn said with a faint voice. "It's important. You'll know later."

The men forced Edwards to stay until everyone had left. Yelling and moving from one room to another, the FBI staff made the situation even more chaotic. Edwards ignored them and forced himself to go to his office to see it looted. One drawer of his office desk lay on the floor. All the others were open and empty.

Edwards searched for the wig in his office. A portion of it was visible protruding from a dossier near the drawer. He picked up the wig and examined it from all sides. The inside was coated in a thin film, which he initially assumed was some sort of protective barrier to prevent allergic reactions. Just as he was about to toss it aside, Quinn's words echoed in his ears: the wig was important and he would explain why.

Walking out of the room with heavy steps, he folded the wig and put it in his jacket pocket. The staff asked for his orders, but Quinn's words still buzzed in his head.

A call from John-Ward made him forget everything about the wig.

"I'll shoot you between the eyes if they kill the man," the President said.

"It's out of our hands, Mr. President," Edwards replied.

"It'll be out of our hands if we lose him," the President said. "If we do, we all must kill ourselves."

Edwards had considered suicide until the wig started to intrigue him. He reached into his pocket and decided it was worth staying alive for one more day.

CHAPTER 15

Waring watched on the TV what seemed to be the largest crowds ever gathered to lynch a Black man.

"It's impossible to rescue him this time," he said.

Things went awry for the White supremacists. They were now Blacks who gathered to lynch a White man in a park named after a slave owner. Color no longer mattered. They were the nation, White and pure-blooded, while he was the wicked Black who beat them with a virus or even black magic.

A platform was quickly erected, and the devil stood on it with his hands tied behind his back. Yells rose from every corner of Gadsdenboro Park to hang the Black Antichrist and rid the chosen ones of the curse he put on them. Others scaled the buildings around the park to avoid missing the event. More people thronged into the Cruise Terminal Parking, now evacuated because of the turmoil. Their jostling to go into the park to see and hear what was going on faced the crowd in the park fighting to keep them back. Then they satisfied themselves by watching the live broadcast on their phones.

The multitudes that arrived late had to maneuver around the streets to get to the Columbus Street Terminal, which was also evacuated, and gather there.

A Black group was approaching. Men in white and women in black moved in a double line toward the platform. They surrounded it in a single circle and said spells to dispel the curse. Quinn recognized them as the warlocks and witches belonging to one of the several magic brotherhoods and sisterhoods. This one had linked itself to The White League. The two last decades saw the spread of witchcraft alongside the rise of White supremacy.

Quinn smiled. "One superstition brings another and another," he said.

He guessed the purpose of their coming. The thing the scientists couldn't achieve, with and without torturing him, those people of illusions wanted to do.

A warlock shouted into the loudspeaker, "You've got no choice but to tell us where you hid your magic."

The mob yelled and applauded.

"You can find the magic yourself, my colleague," Quinn said. His mouth curled up in a smile of irony.

"You better hush your mouth!" a witch said, softly and smiling, though. "It's your magic, not ours."

"Talk!" the other warlocks shouted at him .

Quinn noticed the witches were not angry or saying anything. To his surprise, they were smiling and their eyes shone with admiration in their black faces.

"I hid the magic in a near location, but you can't get it," Quinn replied, his head buzzing with the question about the smiling witches.

The group and the armed men in the greater circle around the platform heard his answer. But the mob imagined he said the place. They yelled again.

And as if the magic was in the square, the master of the magicians turned around. Quinn's smile told him he had said a joke.

"Where?" the man asked in a firm voice.

Quinn nodded to the place of his heart.

"Here," he answered. "You need to get it out."

Feeling that staying more than that would humiliate him, the warlock left the circle and walked to Dylann. He whispered to him that it was their turn to get the secret from the man.

Pretending serenity, the group of magicians left in a double line. The witches turned over their shoulders with the same smile on their faces. Quinn heard one of them saying, "O! How lovely!" Then he understood. He was the only White man and they were still feeling like White women.

The group of people stood at a distance from the platform, their yells growing louder as they called to lynch the devil .

Waring was changing while keeping his eyes fixed on the TV. A hard choice weighed heavily on his mind.

"Will Quinn accept me bargaining with those lunatics?" he asked himself. "But what's the guarantee of setting him free if I told them about the mysterious ray? Maybe I should fake a code supposed to stop the ray. I'd then tell them it's decipherable and rests in yonder Sullivan Island near the code of Poe's Gold Bug story and let them waste their time searching for it."

He opened the door and turned to the TV that he left on. "That's if they do believe in Mercy Ray," he said before pushing the door shut.

When he arrived at the square, Edwards was attempting to make his way through the throngs. Informing the people about his authority was of little use. In some places, they blocked his way with their bodies and he had to maneuver to find a hole. In others, they elbowed him to get back. When he finally got close enough to the platform, he showed Dylann his badge. Dylann beat him on the chest with the butt of his gun.

"Git back!" he ordered him. "We won't let you take our man."

Edwards let out a low cry and scratched his itching chest, but he remained in his place. He counted a few minutes, hoping that people would forget him. Quinn, who was looking at him, wondered if he had brought the wig with him.

Understanding Quinn's glances, Edwards slowly reached into his jacket pocket and took out the wig. He looked the other way and waved the wig near his face as if fanning himself, and wondered how to get the secret of this thing from Quinn.

Suddenly, a loud clamor came from behind, and Edwards turned around to see a wave of people pushing toward the platform.

A huge man shouted, "Let's see if this Black bitch can make him talk."

Quinn's eyes widened in shock. It was Ella, his wife, and a White baby in her arms. The man who shouted was grabbing her by the arm and pushing her forward. They both stopped before the platform.

"We brought her from California," the man thundered.

He pushed her to the ground and leaned forward, then pulled her by the hair and shook her head, looking at Quinn.

"Talk, or I'll strip her naked and let ten men here rape her," he told him before pushing Ella's head down.

Half-prostrating on the ground, Ella turned over her shoulder to the man and then to Quinn.

"This man's not my husband," she cried aloud. "My husband was a Black."

"It's me, Ella," Quinn said. "The baby's ours."

Ella bowed her head until it touched the ground. "But Vesey was Black. He was a Black man," she said, calmly crying.

"I was Black, Ella," Quinn said. "But I'm still the same Vesey. I chose this fate to do a job. And I did it."

Ella looked at the child. She wiped its white face with a hand. Quinn's words pleased her. Now, she became sure the baby was theirs. Tears kept running down her cheeks.

"No more crying, my dear," Quinn said. "Nobody will ever accuse you of sleeping with a White bastard. Our baby bore my altered DNA."

He smiled at her. "Ella, my dear. Look at those crazy hordes," he went on. "They got what they deserved. All hated Black people, but all are now Blacks. I and the baby are White."

Ella raised her head to him and laughed.

"Then everyone will know it's our baby," she said. "No matter if he's White. You're his father."

"And this makes them crazier," he said. "Do you want me to transform you too and make them cry and beat the ground with their heads? Just try to go back to California or any place outside the South. The virus has shifted there."

The huge man darted to the platform and grabbed Quinn's throat with one hand while frowning at him.

"You must transform us back to our color, dirty ape," he said between his teeth. "We'll shoot you then like a mad dog."

Quinn's eyes bulged and his teeth pressed together. He tried to breathe. The man let go and Quinn spat on him. The man wiped his face with his sleeve, looked at Quinn for a few seconds and then slammed him on the face.

Waring had approached the scene, raising both hands to grab their attention.

"Stop it! I know the remedy," he shouted.

The closer people heard him and hushed. The rest continued their noise.

"What secret? And who are you?" Dylann shouted.

Waring gestured toward Quinn. "He told me everything about it," he said. "I'll tell you, but first, let the woman go."

A man with a rifle behind Dylann recognized Waring. "He's the Blacks-loving priest. The people burned his church," he said.

Another man leaned in Dylann's ear, asking if they could trust him.

Dylann gestured toward the armed men surrounding Ella.

"Let her go," he commanded. "One bitch less won't change anything. Two of you take her out of here."

Waring had gotten close to Ella, whispering something to her.

"Hey you," Dylann told Waring. "Don't waste our time. I bet you're an original Nigger but your skin is so thick your friend couldn't transform you to White."

Waring nodded to Ella to go, then looked up at the sky. Quinn's eyes grew wide with fear.

"Don't!" he shouted. "Please don't. Let them kill me. Okay? I'm not afraid."

"Sorry, I promised to talk," Waring said.

Still looking up, he shouted as if performing on stage, "It's something you can't stop. Nobody can stop it. A cosmic ray from an unknown star in a faraway galaxy ".

The crowd began to clamor around him. Waring looked over to Quinn who sighed.

I said I'd tell them, Waring thought to himself, hoping his eyes would convey it. *I didn't say I'd tell them the whole truth.*

"What's the remedy?" Dylann asked. "Say it quickly."

"It's a wig this man wore," Waring answered, pointing to Quinn. He saw disappointment in Quinn's eyes.

Edwards reached into his pocket, intending to quietly leave the scene. Quinn's eyes now were on him. It was time to choose the lesser evil. If the FBI boss took the wig, the scientists would discover its secret.

"Stop that man," Quinn shouted. "He's got the wig. I asked him to keep it."

Dylann needed a moment to understand whom Quinn meant.

"Oh, the biggest bastard of the FBI," he said. "Bring'm here ".

A dozen men stopped Edwards, who pressed his hand on his pocket to secure the wig. The men pushed him toward Dylann. Edwards stood before Dylann and tried to show him his authoritative power.

"You'll pay the price for it," he threatened.

Dylann clouted him in the stomach. Edwards bent over and shut his eyes in pain. A man in the group pushed him to the ground, put a knee on his cheek, and retrieved the wig from his pocket. The man then handed the wig to Dylann, who turned it around and upside down.

"Nothing's extraordinary in this thing," he said, turning toward Waring for an explanation.

Waring held his hand up to him.

"I'll show you," he said calmly.

He took the wig and ascended the few steps of the stairs to the platform.

"Julius, no!" Quinn whispered.

"Yes, Leo," Waring said, lifting the wig above his head and twirling around to show the crowd.

"This wig is made of a special substance that can protect from the cursed ray," he shouted. "It's only one wig. And only one man can use it, and it's up for grabs. Let's see who gets lucky."

With that, he hurled the wig toward the crowd.

The people near the platform jostled to catch it. One jumped and took it. Another snatched it from him. A bunch of them jumped on him and knocked him down to the ground. The brawl escalated as more people rushed in a huge wave and beat everyone in the spot .

Nervously clenching a cigarette between his teeth, Dylann nodded up to his men to retrieve the wig. Ready for the order, they plunged into the crowd, using the butts of their rifles to beat back the mob. The people fought back, trying to seize the guns.

Two of Dylann's men fired shots into the air. It only provoked a fiercer attack, forcing them to retreat to Dylann's side. Dylann aimed his gun at the crowd, spat out his cigarette, and shot a man in the back. His men followed suit, firing indiscriminately at the attackers.

As the armed group swept the mob out of the area, another wave of people attacked the platform, fists and feet flying. In the chaos, Quinn was knocked to the ground, hitting his head on Waring's .

"Only one piece of the alloy is enough to find its secret," Waring shouted to Quinn over the din of the chaos.

"It's protective, not a remedy," Quinn replied.

"Then they'll give its secret to the states outside the Confederacy," Waring said.

"Will they do?"

"Maybe," Waring answered. "But in case they can find it."

"Yes?"

"It's in my pocket," Waring said.

"So they'll find it when they kill us and they'll…. Ouch!"

"Not even then, unless I'm too late."

Before receiving a kick like his friend, Waring struggled to take out the film from his pocket. With a trembling hand, he put it in his mouth and began to chew on it.

"Is it okay now?" he asked, his voice muffled by the film in his mouth.

"Yes, it's safe now," Quinn shouted. "But Ella!"

"She's safe too. I gave her money to go back home. Hey, don't…" Waring trailed off.

The men dragged both Quinn and Waring by their feet in a circle, relentlessly beating them before forcing them back onto their feet. More individuals joined. But with no more room to beat Quinn and Waring, they shouted to hang them.

The two friends were half-dead when two ropes were prepared. A clamor rose from the next side of the park. It was as if the crowd was protesting. They heard swear words. Quinn thought they wanted to have their share. Waring found it out.

Waring caught Quinn's attention, pointing to the distant screen. "Hey, look over yonder," he said.

Quinn followed his gaze. "Where?" he asked, unsure of what to look for.

"The screen ahead," Waring replied.

Quinn turned to the monitor, his eyes widening as he saw the images displayed on it.

"Oh! Is it real?" he asked.

The screen showcased a massive gathering, though Quinn couldn't make out the name of the city. It was evident, however, that it was one outside the Confederacy. The crowd of both Whites and Blacks had come together to demonstrate against White supremacists, chanting "We Shall Overcome."

The crowd in the Park booed in disapproval.

"At last, the silenced spoke," Waring said.

"And the silent knew it was wrong to be silent," Quinn said.

The screen then switched to another city, and the crowd once again erupted into a chorus of boos. The third was an all-Black city. The booing came louder, mixed with insults.

"My God!" Waring exclaimed.

"More Black people there, and a lot of anger here," Quinn said.

"No, my friend," Waring said. "It's not because of the number of Blacks. It's South Carolina, Columbia."

"Columbia?!" Quinn exclaimed.

"It's Resurrection Day," Waring said .

"How many of them are there?" Quinn asked.

"I can't count them," Waring replied. "But there are certainly a lot of them, and that's nuff."

"Genesis eighteen, thirty-two," Quinn said.

Waring thought for a while.

"I can't remember the verse," he said.

"It's carved on my heart," Quinn said. "Abraham pleaded with God to spare Sodom if He found even ten righteous people."

"The majority may still believe it's none of their business," Waring said, "but we can see more than ten."

Louder boos and insults came from all the corners of the Park.

"Now what?" Quinn asked.

"Now also all Blacks," Waring said.

"Another town in South Carolina "?

"Guess what, my friend," Waring said. "It's here. It's Charleston. And look! They're marching to this very park. Twice the mad people here. More than ten people. I expected they'd wake up to their fault. Late, but better than nothing."

He turned to Quinn and noticed he wasn't joyful .

"It's a great change, isn't it?" Waring asked him.

"It is," Quinn answered. "But I wonder why should people suffer to feel the suffering of others?"

The camera zoomed in on the face of a Black woman in the front row, her fist raised and shouting anti-racist slogans.

"And here's another surprise," Waring said.

"Yeah," Quinn responded, as if in a daze. "That's Ashley, the devil's widow. She's leading the revolution."

The park became more agitated. Waring spotted a man rushing toward them as if trying to arrive at the last minute.

"An angel coming to our rescue," he said.

"No, he's Satan's agent in the media," Quinn said. "Zach Martin."

Zach shoved his way through the crowd to get to the platform.

"Your last report about us?" Quinn asked him.

"I'm here the butcher, not the reporter," Zack answered, his breath shortened.

"The first bastard to die," Zach said, putting the rope around Waring's neck.

Waring turned to Quinn and whispered through the blood in his mouth, "He should've hanged you first. You were the Black and you brought it to them."

"It's the subconscious, my friend," Quinn replied. "They see only the color. Their brain is located right in their eyes."

Zach slammed him in the face and put the noose around his neck.

"The marching army of conscience will be too late," Quinn said. "Hey, Zach. I want to tell the people here and there about Mercy Ray. It's your last opportunity."

Zach slammed him again, cutting him off.

"Keep it to yourself, you Nigger with white patches," he said.

Quinn didn't give up. "I can redirect the ray back here and undo the change it caused."

Zack responded by striking him in the stomach.

"Your lies won't save your life, dirty dog," he said.

"It's no use, bro," Waring said.

"It's no use," Quinn echoed.

The pain made Quinn think of the possibility of six-month seasons of white and black, one after the other. He couldn't think of anything else except for the fact that Zack had taken even the smallest chance away from his people.

Quinn looked up, "Father Waring! You remember something?"

"Nothing for now," Waring answered.

"You're a priest," Quinn said. "Say the prayers before we die."

Waring began to pray. Zack kicked the stool from under his feet, then Quinn's. They were left hanging.

The shouts of the Black crowd shook the park. One group started singing "God Save the South." The rest joined in.

"God save the South from you," Quinn gasped.

"Racism is a chronic sin," Waring managed to say. "God save our souls. God save the South."

Quinn tried to turn southward to look at the sky. A kick from Zack helped him. Quinn remembered Waring's speech about the will of God fulfilled by His enemies. He thought of himself as a tool of God's will and hoped he was a good tool.

Quinn's heart stopped beating while his eyes remained fixed on the satellite .

The crowds cheered and said swear words, waved their flags and swung them, chanted their anthems and danced. They clenched their fists and waited for the protesters to come and attack them.

Unaware of the events on Earth, the satellite remained in the sky, silent and calm and reflecting Mercy Ray.

www.ingramcontent.com/pod-product-compliance
Lightning Source LLC
Chambersburg PA
CBHW022130150726
47992CB00002B/525